CW01267045

BORN AGAIN

A CHARLIE STONE NOVEL

TREVOR TWOHIG

Born Again: A Charlie Stone Novel

www.trevortwohig.com
tjtwohig1@yahoo.co.uk

ISBN: 9798409765682

1st Edition 2022

BORN AGAIN

A CHARLIE STONE NOVEL

TREVOR TWOHIG

1

There are many things they don't tell you about having babies.
The first one is that it is unwise to encourage a woman in labour to 'push.' In a way, this really highlights the main differences between men and women. Charlie thought saying ‘push’ would be the most logical thing to do in this situation, however, he soon realised it was not, given the foul-mouthed tirade of abuse that followed from his wife, Tara.
In short, do not believe what the movies tell you.
Morwenna, the thickset African nurse, looked at Tara's vagina and shook her head.
'No, not quite yet.'
In fact you hear, ‘don't push,’ more than ‘push’ as far as Charlie was concerned. He wanted to be present for the birth of his second child, his wife’s first, but felt like a stunt double in a rom-com.
Useless.
While Tara was red-faced, hair stuck to her head and in severe discomfort, he sat trying to look busy, helpful and engaged.
'Not yet,' Morwenna repeated.
Charlie gripped Tara's hand tighter as she moved from her side and onto her back to try to get comfortable. He accidentally saw her vagina. Unrecognisable.
'Don’t look down there! What did I say?' Tara bellowed.
‘Sorry,' Charlie said, bringing his eyes back to her torso. Normally he was told off for looking there too, but nothing about today was ‘normal.’
Tara puffed on the oxygen mask, long deep breaths.

He looked at the far wall of the warm, labour room. There were pictures of small colourful birds, maybe three of them, surrounded and swallowed up by the hospital paint job. Medicinal magnolia.
'Here it comes again...' Tara said ruefully, gripping Charlie's hand tighter.

At the front of the building, a man had parked his car in the drop-off zone.
He wasn't supposed to do this, but he had. For a hospital the size of the William Harvey in Ashford, the drop off area was a joke. Like a number of services in the NHS, it was not really fit for purpose. He looked shiftily around and knew that no one would challenge him at 5am on a Sunday morning.
He closed the car door quietly and made his way to the entrance. He nodded at the 'temperature checker' on the door as she raised the plastic gun to his head. He smiled, she nodded.
Normally she asked if they had an appointment. She didn't this time.
The man walked through the hospital and towards the Folkestone Ward.
He was about five foot five inches, wore a sand-coloured Stone Island jacket, and knew precisely where he was going.

'I can't do this! I need a caesarean, I *need* one!'
Morwenna reassuringly rubbed Tara's arm.
'OK, the doctor is busy now, but I will tell him.'
'Find him *now!* I need a caesarean. The pethidine is putting me to sleep, I have no energy...' Tara trailed off.
'OK, darling. Try not to have too much of the gas and

air. This makes you sleepy too.'
'Oh my God, I can feel him...' Tara said. 'He's moving down.'
Charlie tried not to look, but it was impossible. The pulsing pineapple was now a wispy watermelon. He could see how romance took a kick in the shins after childbirth. *Totally.* He cursed his mind for having such inappropriate thoughts during this time, and refocused.
'Ah, yes. He is coming. Wait for contraction, then push!' Morwenna said.
'Oh, Christ. Fucking hell, *Charlie!*'

The man in the Stone Island jacket walked nonchalantly up to the door of the ward.
There wasn't a soul about. It usually was empty this time of the week, early in the morning.
He pressed the silver button for entry and waited. There was no answer.
He looked along the corridor, beyond the locked doors; there was no sign of movement. He pressed the buzzer and waited against the wall.

'Right, your baby is coming...' Morwenna said, moving from second gear into third. Charlie was pretty certain there were no more gears in Wenna's repertoire.
Tara let out a sound that came from the depths of her stomach, beyond the soul. Like an animal's screech; deep and visceral.
Charlie watched her whole-body shake. It had dawned on them both that the caesarean would not be forthcoming. Nor the epidural. It was her and her alone and the shortest distance between two points

was a straight line.
She was marching.
'Push with the contraction, do not waste it!' Morwenna said, as Tara growled, shuddered and drove her abdomen forward.
With a remarkable movement, a human life emerged, like a pop-pass from a rugby player and landed in Wenna's arms, squawking like a baby bird.
Charlie was bleary-eyed and in awe.
Tara relaxed back into the bed from which she appeared to be hovering above previously. The moments were in slow-mo, like stop motion and when it ended, Charlie's daughter was nestling into Tara's chest.

'Sorry, it's just so busy at the moment. Who are you here to see?'
This was good news for the man.
A doctor.
They wore different colour scrubs here, red.
They had far less of a handle on who came in and out, as it wasn't on their heads if there was ever an issue. That would fall on the nurses and the midwives, who clearly were too busy to worry about anything other than what was directly in front of them.
The doctor placed her badge on top of the scanner to unlock the door, nodded and held the door open for the man.
He entered, past the admin desk at the end of the corridor. It remained unmanned, but the wards were bustling with activity. Someone was in trouble and there was a birth occurring across the way.
'Oh, god. It's OK, I'm coming...' the doctor said before sprinting off towards the melee.

This was going well.
He turned right at the end of the corridor and checked the rooms. There were women lying in their beds.
One was feeding her child, most were asleep.
He turned to the individual rooms on his right. He went to the second one and pushed the handle down.
There was a woman lying in bed.
Her eyes were open as the man entered. He nodded at her.
She smiled and nodded at him.
He picked up the baby that lay in a small plastic cot at the foot of her bed.
He looked at her again. She nodded, approvingly.
She passed him a small bag that she'd made up for him.
He held the baby to his chest, grabbed the bag and left the room.
In the corridor, the nurse on the admin desk had returned, but didn't look up. The man still shushed the baby, as if it was his, as if he was invested in the little ball of flesh. The nurse couldn't have cared less what he was doing; he could have been armed with Semtex and C4 singing insurgent anthems for all she cared.
He rounded the corner and made his way to the exit. He stood at the door and pressed the buzzer to be let out. His heart sped up slightly, anxious that the nurse might quiz him, or a midwife may be coming in from the other ward.
The door buzzed open. *Easy – peasy.*
The third pick up this week.
Experience told him that once he was out of the ward, the job was done.
No one asked questions outside in the main hospital

building.
The baby was crying now.
He looked at it and laughed. Laughed at its silly scrunched up face, its little green woolly hat.
He had learned that meant the baby was healthy and had no post-natal issues. That's why he never took the ones with the red hats. He put the baby in the car seat he had pre-prepared and drove off into the night.

2

The baby's hair was soft like golden candyfloss. Charlie noticed that there was a perpetual squawk coming from her little mouth, and that she was covered in red goo that was somewhat disconcerting. Morwenna gently wiped the baby, while smiling. Her firm strokes seemed too rough for such a precious bundle, but Charlie knew better than to say anything. The baby continued to shout her raucous little song, until she was back on Tara's chest. Tara was smiling, and whispering to her newborn. Tears were in her eyes. Pure joy. She reached for Charlie's hand who moved around the side of the bed and leaned into Tara's long blonde hair.

'Are you OK?'

Tara nodded. Charlie pulled away, anxious, not wanting to hurt his wife, who he presumed would be somewhat fragile.

'You want to hold her?' Tara asked, carefully moving her fingers around the tiny bundle.

'Erm, no.... I uh...'

Tara looked a little perturbed.

'It's OK. You won't break her, look...' Morwenna intervened, picking up the baby. 'Hold her like this.'

She passed Charlie the little girl and he put her on his chest nervously. He noticed that she smelt like butter, but immediately settled when he put her to his chest. After a few moments, he looked back at Tara who had her eyes shut, as she rested on the bed.

'Here, let me pop her on the scales,' Morwenna said, taking the baby.

'Go, have a walk and take a drink,' Morwenna said.

'Can you bring me a snack and some water?' Tara

said, her eyes still closed as she drifted between dream world and reality.
'Sure. Do you need anything?' He asked Morwenna.
'No, it's fine. Take a minute, get some air.' She smiled at him.
'OK.' He didn't want to leave his wife and child, but Tara was about to sleep and Morwenna was certainly a safer pair of hands than he was at this point.
He went over to the Costa café and grabbed a black coffee for himself and a slice of cake and water for Tara.
Towards the front of the hospital was a small shop that sold cold drinks, teddies, puzzles and papers.
Charlie looked at the front page of the dailies.
The popular papers ran stories about the prime minister, politics and whom he had or hadn't paid to decorate his Westminster flat.
Charlie was uninterested.
On the front of the Daily Comet, a publication, renowned for its far-fetched story lines and propensity for half-naked ladies, ran a story that tickled him.
'Alien spacecraft hidden under English seaside town?'
As the elation of childbirth flooded him with endorphins, he decided to pick up the paper and have a quick read, chuckling to himself. He still found it mind boggling that although these stories that made this paper were clearly fabricated, the paper still was in print and very successful. *'Crash landing in the sixties, secret officials working day and night to uncover secrets of far away galaxies…'*
Charlie put it back and surmised that the boobs and bums that are selling the paper.

He picked up a more reputable broadsheet: *HGV Driver shortages, food shortages, fuel crises…* it was depressing what Brexit had done to the UK.
Not wanting the state of the country to harsh his buzz, Charlie walked back to the maternity ward, trying hard not to spill hot, black coffee over his hand.
He pressed the button and waited. There were nurses walking through the corridors inside, but no one was coming to the door. He pressed again, this time harder and longer. As he did, he dropped the thick black liquid onto the floor.
'Dammit!' he said under his breath, before reaching back to the buzzer. Before he could though, the door whizzed open.
'Can I help you?'
'Yes, sorry. My wife has just given birth, room 1, Tara Stone…'
'Right, OK.'
Charlie was already at the door of the room and saw Tara lying on the bed, lightly stirring.
Morwenna and the baby were nowhere to be seen.

Steve parked the car and went to the backseat. The baby was sleeping now as he unfastened the car chair that he was lying in.
He looked both ways to make sure he was fully alone before carrying the car seat through the large green gates of the warehouse and towards the dim light of the building in front of him.
Steve's brother, Johnny, greeted him at the door, taking the baby seat from him.
'Careful with that,' Steve whispered.
'Jesus, fat little bastard,' Johnny used his second hand to steady the chair before placing it on the metal

worktop.
'Ah, come on now. The car seat is what's heavy. In fact, that is a gap in the market… I know you like to exercise your entrepreneurial spirit.'
'What gap in the market?'
'Making a car seat that is not cripplingly heavy when it has a baby in it!' Steve said.
Johnny sighed.
'Perhaps it's the cheap, shitty car seats you buy.'
'A car seat is a car seat. And they are all far too heavy.'
The baby started gurgling.
'What time is the wizard arriving?'
'Twenty minutes.'
'Got any milk? Nappies?'
'I didn't have time to stop off. In addition, I don't particularly want to draw any attention. The local press have yet to notice what's happening.'
'Right.' Steve said as the baby started to cry.
'Missing mummy already?' Johnny laughed a deep, sinister laugh.
'Don't be like that. It's not very becoming.' Steve said.
Johnny approached the baby and placed his pinkie into his mouth. The baby started making a sucking sound and immediately quietened down.
'It's a bit weird how much you love babies.' Johnny said.
'It's not *weird*. I have just a natural predisposition to helping those more vulnerable than us. Anyway, it's you who has the right fingers for this job. He could bite through that little finger and it would still be twice the size of most people's!'
'Now, now. No need to get jealous over my bell ringers, son. These bad boys come in handy with the

ladies if you catch my drift. I am sure your tiny little kid hands come in some use too. I mean, they must make your boyfriend's cock look bigger...'
The sound of the metal gate opening, gained the men's attention. A man that the McCarthys were not expecting walked into their courtyard.
'Is this your man?' Johnny asked.
'Nope…'
'Good evening. My name is Leon, the wizard has sent me on his behalf.'
'Where is he then?' Johnny asked.
'I am afraid he has requested the company of Stephen. On his own.'
Johnny and Steve looked at one another.
'Oh, like that is it, little brother?' Johnny replied as Steve shrugged his shoulders. 'Right, well then. Off you fuck.'
Steve went with the new man, Leon, out of the metal gates and around to the left of their facility towards the East Cliff.
'Have you got milk for him?' Steve asked.
'Of course! Does he need it now?' Leon asked.
Steve had placed his finger in the baby's mouth after Johnny. He took it out and the bubba immediately started wailing.
'I see. Pass him here.'
Steve carefully passed the baby to him.
Leon held him as the little baby greedily sucked on the bottle in his hand.
'I better get back to Johnny…'
'The wizard is just in the car up here.'
Steve followed and opened the passenger door to the black Mercedes that was parked by the side of the road. The wizard was in the back and smiled at Steve

as he sat down in front.
'Great work, Stephen. Very, very good indeed.'
'No worries. But, uh, what's this about?'
'Oh, I think it's for the best, I just deal with you in this... business...'
'Yeah, but Johnny's my brother. My partner.'
The wizard laughed.
'Of course. But... for now, this is the way it will be,' the wizard said calmly.
'So, what shall I tell him?' Steve asked.
'It's not important. What is important is that nothing comprises the work we do here. OK?'
Steve nodded, before exiting the car and heading back to his brother.

3

'Where's the baby?' Charlie shouted.

Tara awoke from her dream state with a start.

She looked around.

'They took her to get her weighed and measured, Charlie…' She put her hand out and gestured for him to come to her, but he was out of the room and up the corridor, checking in each of the rooms.

There was screaming and bellowing from room one, where a woman writhed on a bed and a man in a black t-shirt, with spiky hair, looked at the floor, forlorn.

He saw Charlie poke his head in and immediately started giving words of encouragement to the woman, while Charlie exited.

Room two was empty and Tara was stirring in room three.

In between the labour rooms was an office, Charlie pushed the door open and found Morwenna and another midwife laying his baby daughter on a set of large scales.

They saw the panic in his eyes.

'Everything OK, Mr. Stone?' Morwenna said.

He calmed. The red mist left.

'Yes. Yes, sorry. I just...'

'I will bring the baby girl back to you,' Morwenna ushered him out.

Rather than return to Tara, he waited outside the door. It was the only way in or out and he wasn't taking any chances here.

After a few moments, Morwenna appeared with the baby swaddled and looking cosy.

Charlie thrust his arms towards her and the midwife

handed him the bundle.
She passed her over and Charlie gratefully accepted. As she placed her in his arms, Charlie noticed that the baby was wearing a bright red hat.
'Does she need that hat on?' He asked.
'Yes, Mr Charlie I… come back to the room and I will explain.'
Tara was sitting upright in bed and after Charlie entered, she visibly relaxed.
Morwenna shut the door behind them and indicated for Charlie to sit down.
'So, we have done the initial tests on the baby and you know, the baby is healthy and looking good. However, we have noticed that there is a slight hernia on the baby's navel...'
'Hernia? What do you mean?' Tara interjected.
'It is not a problem, for now. There just might be some issues with the stomach and we will need to keep a close on the baby's digestion, as she gets bigger. The paediatrician will want to meet her tomorrow morning and check her over.'
There was silence from the two parents.
'It is OK; we just need to be careful, especially in these early days. We are going to move you to the Folkestone Ward, this afternoon. You must keep this hat on your daughter, so the doctors know that he needs to check her.'
'OK.' Charlie said.
Tara nodded in agreement.
Morwenna left the room and shut the door behind her.
Tara's eyes filled with tears, this time they were ones of sadness.
'Let's not worry, hey? It sounds like it's something fairly…'

'… What? A hernia, in our baby's stomach?'
'I mean, when… yeah, I guess it doesn't sound great when you put it like that. But, she is in the right place.' Charlie said softly.
'Pass her here, please.' Tara asked and Charlie duly obliged.
'There is no point in you staying here for now, hun…' Tara said.
'… Oh no, I'm happy to…'
'Listen, go home. Get some rest and bring back some fresh clothes… and some decent food!' Tara smiled.
Charlie leaned in and hugged her. There was the scent of sweat, mixed with a sweetness he hadn't recognised before.
'Careful, you don't want to squash baby Ridley!'
Tara looked at Charlie to gauge his reaction. After a moment, he smiled and nodded.
'*Ridley*… I like it.'
'It means chosen one. Now skidaddle Mister and get some rest.' Tara smiled and Charlie did precisely as he was told.
The cool December air hit him like an avalanche. He had become too accustomed to the grim warm stench of the hospital ward.
He had a bit of a walk around to the car which he had moved and parked up a side street, as he was not keen on paying the hospital car park prices, given he had no idea how long he would be in there for.
He pulled out his mobile phone, but as he did, a man walking the other way knocked his arm. Charlie's phone fell clean out of his hand and luckily, into the grass at the side of the road.
'Oh my word, sorry pal.' The man said, leaning down to pick it up for him. Charlie noticed his stone island

jacket and smiled.
The man handed him the phone.
'You a football fan?' Charlie asked.
'Course. Mighty Irons.' The man said. Charlie nodded.
'I'll let you off,' he winked at the man.
The man cocked his head, sizing Charlie up. He clearly didn't take Charlie's comment in the jokey way he meant it.
Eventually his deep blue eyes softened.
'Yeah, no worries.' He said, and moved quickly towards the entrance of the hospital.

Charlie bustled into his house, busy and preoccupied. His mind was always in about four places at once.
Firstly, he felt bad that he wasn't at the hospital with Tara. Secondly, he wanted to know what was wrong with the baby, but he also knew what hospitals were like. It would be hurry up and wait all day, and they probably wouldn't get any information until later. Not that he begrudged the nurses; they were run off their feet. He would check in later of course.
Charlie also was preoccupied with his work situation that was a little precarious to say the least.
He had officially left the police force, but hadn't fully begun any other role yet.
He wanted to start up a private investigation firm, but he also wanted to go into schools and teach criminology seminars.
Neither had got off the ground, what with the pregnancy and so on.
Also, tomorrow would be one year sober for Charlie.
This was weighing on his mind and causing him severe anxiety.

It was as if the closer he got to the milestone, the desire to drink and the cravings increased ten-fold.
Upstairs now, Charlie disrobed and jumped in the shower.
After thirty seconds or so, he turned the temperature to cold and waited for the icy prickles to pierce his bruised and scarred skin.
He shuddered and breathed deeply in and out, controlling the urge to whip the warm back on.
Once out, he dried himself quickly with a towel before getting dressed in the master bedroom.
Tara had placed a large, full-length mirror in the room and he was able to take a good look at himself. It had been a while since he could, without recoiling in either guilt or disgust. He had escaped some close scrapes and his body told that tale all too well.
Grazes, bruising and scars fell across his torso and back, but despite the outwardly grisly appearance, he had healed. Apart from the odd twinge here and there, he felt as good as he had done for years.
His face was unscathed and due to his abstinence from alcohol, was clear and defined, where before it had been a little pink and puffy. For the first time in decades, he wasn't using any hair products. Without wanting to sound like a TV commercial, all he needed to do was push it with his hand to the side and that would be that these days.
His eyes were clear, not glassy. There was the customary bags under the eyes, he couldn't do anything about those, except use his wife's make up, but as much as he wanted to look good, at some things he drew the line.
His phone buzzed and he picked it up from the bed.
'Hello?'

'Hi, Charlie. It's Becky.'
'Hey, Bex! How's it going?'
'Good. Good. I mean, a bit slow, but… anyway how are you? T had a baby yet?'
'Yes… yes she has…'
'Oh, congratulations, Charlie!' Becky said, with what Charlie could only describe as mock-sincerity.
'Yeah, thanks. She is still in the hospital. She has given me a free pass though while she rests and does all the boring stuff. '
'Lucky you! In fact that's the reason that I called. I have a lead here that you may want to investigate… but… I guess it may not be quite the right time?'
Charlie pondered this.
His plan had been to work in partnership with Becky at the investigation agency that he was supposed to be starting.
'… I mean, it hasn't really been the right time for the last few weeks, so I guess…' Becky continued.
'… All right Bex, stop riding me would you? You know I have had a lot on…'
'Well Tara has, you have just been sitting around twiddling your thumbs according to her...' Becky sniggered down the phone.
Charlie smiled.
Perhaps he was procrastinating.
Perhaps he was enjoying his sobriety and his redundancy package a little too much recently.
'… In fact, maybe I should start the new firm on my own, come to think about it…'
'Whatever. What's this so-called lead you are on about then?' Charlie said curtly. Caught between the joke and the burning reality that he did need to do something productive with his life.

'I think you should come and see it, meet me on the beach… that's if you've got time?'
Charlie sighed, checking his watch.
'Give me half an hour, all right?'

4

Charlie picked up the phone and rang Tara.

'Hey, handsome.' She sounded sleepy, and he felt a stab of guilt for waking her up.

He was keen to keep her informed of his whereabouts, so that she didn't worry about him. He had learned from when he was a copper in homicide, that the dangerous situations took their toll on Tara.

She also decided it would be a good idea to talk through some of their hard and fast rules when they got back together a few months ago. She made it very clear that she wanted to be integral to Charlie's life, whether it was dangerous or not.

'I'm sorry, did I wake you?'

'It's OK, Charlie, is everything all right?' she yawned into the phone.

'Yes, I'm fine I just wanted to know whether there was any news about the baby…'

'… Ridley, Charlie! Her name's Ridley!'

'Yes, sorry. Any news on Ridley?'

'No, not really. They moved me to the Folkestone Ward, which… If I'm honest, it is a bit of a shame really. There are five other mothers with newborns here.'

'Oh, blimey.' Charlie imagined the endless wailing and shuddered. 'But, our baby is OK?'

'She's fine, Charlie. I am definitely going to be here overnight though. They are run off their feet and the pediatrician hasn't checked her over yet.'

'Oh right, OK. That is… well… I'll pop back a bit later, yeah?'

'That would be great. Bring me some chocolate, maybe?'

'Of course, just...make sure you don't leave her alone, OK?'
'What? Of course not...'
'I mean, even if you need a wee, or a drink... take her with you, yeah?'
'Charlie, of course I will! Relax! I Love you.'
'Love you too.'
Charlie sighed. It wasn't ideal to be without Tara, she had become his rock recently, but then, it couldn't be helped.
He grabbed the car keys from the side and headed out to his battered old Ford Focus.
Charlie took the M20 down to junction 11 and came into Folkestone via Hythe and along the seafront. He wanted to check out the flats at the esplanade, in particular, the one that Tara and Troy shared for four months, not so long ago.
Charlie slowed almost to a stop and he could see that nothing had changed in the top floor apartment suite.
It was still a mess of burnt wood and smashed glass. A police investigation going nowhere.
Charlie could see directly in, where the windows had shattered, presumably due to the pressure of the fire that swept through the upmarket abode. He could just make out the green sofa that had sat pride of place, he presumed, in the middle of the room. It was barely recognisable as most of it was now a dark, charcoal grey.
'We now have a Laura Ashley sofa, *Charlie.*' Tara had once boasted, he remembered thinking that he could not remember what had happened to the woman he fell in love with, as she nestled down with Troy, Charlie's nemesis, on their brand new 'Laura Ashley sofa.'

The security guard who was monitoring the remains of the building, moved towards Charlie, his face scrunched up in a ball, ready for a fight.
Charlie thought better of it and headed onwards towards Folkestone.
As he approached the beach, he felt a pang of… he wasn't sure what.
It was like anxiety, a trigger.
He wanted a drink.
He used the techniques he was shown, tapping his wrist three times, taking a deep breath and letting the overwhelming urge to get wasted, dissipate.
He opened his eyes again and made a mental note to find an AA meeting later today.
He parked the car by the seafront and continued on foot towards the beach. It was breezy, yet not cold and while there were people moving around, by Folkestone's standards, the afternoon was quiet.
As Charlie walked down the concrete slope and onto the beach, he noticed Becky sitting under the esplanade, in one of the coves towards the back of the beach.
'Howdy, stranger,' she said, a smile spreading across her face.
Charlie couldn't help but smile when he saw her.
'Oh come on, give us a hug,' she said as he sat down beside her.
'How are you?' she asked.
'Good, pretty happy really. I am a dad again,' Charlie said, looking out to sea.
'Once more with feeling, Charlie!' Becky mocked.
'No, trust me. I am happy. Of course, just tired, you know…'
'…And lacking a bit of purpose? Wondering where

your life is headed? Feeling downbeat and bored and…'

'…Yes, thanks, I get it. Anyway, why have you dragged me down here?'

Becky looked at Charlie and smiled.

'You'll see.' She said, 'How's Tara?'

'She's good. Recovering. Sleeping…'

'… I mean, how are you and her? Been a bit weird, I guess. The whole Troy thing and…'

'… Yeah, I mean. It's baby steps. I… you know, still struggling to trust her at times, but I do love her, so…'

Becky looked down at the floor and smiled.

'I guess that's all that's really important, hey?' She punched him on the arm. 'Oh look, here we go.' Becky checked her watch, 'right on time.'

She squinted out to sea, before picking up a pair of binoculars that were by her side.

Charlie looked out to where she aimed them and saw a small, black dinghy, bobbing towards the Kentish coastline. Becky passed him the binoculars. He looked through and saw that there were at least eight people packed onto the tiny boat.

'Every day, there is a new boat filled with immigrants. Syria, Afghanistan, Iraq, Iran, Lebanon, Eritria… you name it they turn up in their droves.'

'OK…'

'That's not the interesting part. The interesting part is what happens to them when they land ashore. Hold tight.'

Charlie watched for what seemed like an age as the plastic boat pulled nearer to the shore. There were very few members of the public on the beach, but there were shouts of derision from one couple who

were playing frisbee with their child. Another woman and her son packed up and left. Charlie noticed that there were pro-refugee supporters up by the mermaid. One had a sign that read: Welcome! The other had a t-shirt that said, 'trade racists for refugees.'
The coastguard pulled onto the beach just as the boat came ashore. The air was filled with sounds of yelping and wailing.
'My son, my son!' one of the women wailed as she climbed off the boat and fell to her knees. One of the men behind her carried the body of a young boy. He could only have been three or four years old. He laid the boy down on the wet sand, as the howls of the grieving mother cleared the beach of any final stragglers except the coastguard, Charlie and Becky.
'Why are we watching this?' Charlie asked, a little perturbed at the scene.
'Wait for it…'
As the coastguard slowly approached the refugees, the sounds of motorbikes in the distance drew nearer. The coastguard stopped and waited as two motorbikes came down the ramp and onto the beach. The bikers nodded at the coastguard and two of the male refugees got onto each bike after brief discussion, and they hurtled back across the beach and up the ramp.
Once they disappeared, the sound of a police siren briefly pierced the air, as the rest of the group, three women and two children were taken away by Border Control as the police watched on. The mother of the boy had to be dragged away by an officer, as she screamed in desperation. The coastguard waited with the body.
'Well, thanks for that, Bex,' Charlie said sarcastically.

'Come on, Char. Don't tell me that's not a bit strange?'
'Well, yeah. What do you think is going on?'
'I have heard a few things... the jungle grapevine... that the McCarthy brothers are behind it...'
'Behind what? The men being separated?'
Becky nodded solemnly.
'But why?'
'Soldiers for the gang maybe? Putting them to work? Who knows? But don't you want to find out?'
Charlie looked at Becky. 'You know I have just had a baby, right?'
She smiled. 'People have babies and still work!'
Charlie sat pensively.
'Hm. Well, I guess we have our first case then, don't we?' Charlie smiled.
Becky jumped up off the sand and headed up towards the ramp.
'Excellent, let's get cracking then!'

5

The young woman wore a black leather skirt, stockings and little brown pixie boots.
Johnny tried to stop a smile but couldn't.
She ruffled her hair and looked away from him, trying to deflect the awkwardness. She wasn't used to someone like *him*, wanting someone like *her*. She stood with her legs slightly open, inviting. She knew what she was doing; she had done it before with men. The awkward first date type thing.
Although she had known Johnny for years, this was the first *date*.
'Let's get on our toes shall we?'
'Sure, Johnny. I'm ready.' She purred.
He turned and looked back at her in disbelief.
'Are you serious? You call that ready?' Johnny's brow furrowed.
The girl looked lost. Then his face changed.
'Only messing, come on. Cabs here,' he smiled.
'Funny fucker, you.' She said, putting her hand on his back affectionately.
Johnny opened the door for her and she slid into the backseat of the car.

'The problem with Folkestone is it don't know what it is, Johnny. All the dross and fucking dregs of humanity wash up, yet your sitting in a wannabe fucking London posh boy restaurant...' Ron said from across the table.
Johnny nodded.
Steve looked irritated, got up, and went to the toilet. Ron looked at Johnny and smiled, tapping his nose.

'Less of that in public.'
'Sorry, Johnny.'
Across the table, the three girls chatted with one another. They all looked different, yet similar. Their hair was different colours but styles were the same. Their lips were big and their make-up bigger. *It was a thing, wasn't it?* Johnny thought. *These birds look like blow up dolls. What happened to the natural look?*
'It's transitioning, Ron. While everyone looks to the harbour and to gaffs like this, our thing can stay, you know... under wraps.'
Ron nodded.
'The system we have now works for everyone and really while the Border Patrol and Old Bill are barely able to keep up, we can continue to keep going. Right?'
Steve returned to the table.
'Yeah course, Johnny. I mean, it's just...'
'Here, what about your thing? Hospital...?'
Steve nodded at his brother.
'Yeah, good. It is an earner, put it that way. Up to one a week, three bags every...'
The girl who Johnny had brought to the dinner, collapsed in a cacophony of laughter. Her hair was over her face and she was snorting like a micro pig she so wished that she would one day own.
'Are you fucking sure?'
'Sorry Johnny. It's just something that she said.... oh my days...'
Johnny shot her an icy glance, before looking back to his brother. His brother continued talking, but before he could finish his sentence, the girls were off again, this time all three of them howling like wolves.
Johnny's eyes fell dark and without taking his eyes

from his brother, he grabbed the girl by the head, and thrust her face full throttle into the table.

There was a collective gasp from the room.

Ron and Steve got up and began to usher Johnny to the door.

The other girls were screaming with hands over their mouths, watching as the girl lifted her head from the smashed china in front of her.

Blood dripped from her face, a mixture of claret, snot and tears.

Johnny was out the door and into the car before the waiter had reached the table.

Ron pulled the car away slowly, so as not to draw attention, but said nothing.

Steve was in the front seat, Johnny in the back.

'It would be nice to have at least one place where we can have a bite to eat in this town…'

'Drop it out will you. You are my little bro, I don't need you grilling me. These fucking women…'

'Yeah, I mean how dare she laugh?' Steve said, looking over to Ron, hoping he would join in the joke. He didn't.

'Head to the coastline will you, Ron?' Johnny asked.

'Anyway, you were telling us about the hospital, Stephen.' Ron resumed.

'Yeah, like I said it seems to be working. The contact is a bit of a funny fucker. Doesn't like anyone knowing anything, very secretive. But he's like… it's hard to describe really, a calmness… like nothing phases him, you know?'

'I would like to get to know him a bit better,' Johnny announced.

'Well, I don't think that's a great idea. I don't want to sound funny, but he's happy. He likes it the way it is,

he doesn't want anyone else knowing…'
'… However, I *do* know. It's *my* thing.' Johnny returned.
'Well, it's *our* thing. I just… I don't want to be funny, but you know…' Steve struggled, as Ron pulled the car to the side of the road.
'Here, that's your Romanian friend Andrei, innit?' Ron squinted into the distance.
Steve stopped talking immediately and watched the large man, talk to a young boy on a bicycle.
'He's one of ours, Stephen.'
'So he fucking is.'
Johnny and Ron got out of the car and slowly made their way towards the Romanian man who spied them too late. As the boy skidded off on his BMX, Ron grabbed Andrei by the scruff of the neck, while Johnny weighed into the large, fat Albanian man.
Steve watched from the front seat of the car, listening to the forlorn wails.
'Johnny that will do mate,' Ron said.
But the red mist had descended and there was a darkness behind Johnny's eyes, he couldn't be torn off the fat man who was now not responding.
'Johnny!' Art shouted.
Steve looked out of the window of the car and saw the gooey mess that had been made of Andrei. He squinted to check for signs that he was still alive.
He couldn't tell.
'That'll do. We still haven't had dinner yet.' Steve said, as his brother returned to earth, the eyes found their colour, and he returned slowly to the car.
'You could do with skipping a few meals, dear brother of mine.' Johnny said, spitting on the floor as he walked back to the vehicle.

‘What I have noticed is that the refugees coming in, keep getting intercepted, like you saw today. It’s happening more often than you think.’ Becky said, as the pair walked along Fisherman’s Wharf.
‘They come in on the boats, a couple get detained by Border Patrol, the police don’t seem to do anything while what looks like the McCarthy boys disappear with the rest of them.’
‘Hm.’ Charlie said, piqued but unwilling to show his hand to his wily apprentice just yet.
He took his phone from his pocket and speed-dialled a number.
‘Hello Jacko. How have you been?’ Charlie said warmly.
‘Good, my old friend. Phoning me to tell me you want back in? We have got loads of work on here!’ Jacko said, half in jest, fully knowing that once Charlie Stone had made a decision that was that. When he left the police force, it was not a decision he took lightly. He did, however, know that he wasn’t going back to deal with the mountains of admin and paperwork… the bureaucracy that stopped proper crimes being solved.
‘Thanks for the offer but…’
‘… But you are off having babies and living in post-marital bliss? I know, I know… that reminds me, isn’t that baby due soon?’ Jacko remembered.
‘Yep, she has just been born. Baby Ridley.’
‘Congratulations, Charlie! How is Tara doing?’
‘Yeah, good. Just resting at the hospital.’
‘OK, well don’t neglect her like you usually do and get your head all mixed up in…. whatever it is you’re doing now…’ Jacko trailed off. Charlie took a sharp

intake of breath. Jacko's words, although true, were a bit too close to the bone, and reminded Charlie of what had happened a year ago, and how he nearly lost the woman that he loved.

'Yeah, so I just wanted to ask you about something…'

'Fire away… I'm just about to open a bottle of Heineken Zero and stick on the TV, so you're not interrupting anything here…' Jacko chuckled, but he sounded lonely. Charlie felt another stab in the heart. He had neglected his old friend.

'Yeah so, are you involved at all in the boats that are coming in every day, on the beach?'

'What the illegals? Not really. Funny one that. They want us to be there, like a police presence when the boats arrive, but then it all goes through Inland Security and the Border Patrol.'

'So… when the boats arrive, what happens? If you don't mind me asking?'

'Well, they want us there at first, in case there is any trouble or you know… but it became clear that these guys don't want trouble, they just want a chance. Now we sometimes send a car if we have one in the area, but it's all Border Patrol and other…. um… outside agencies…'

'Outside agencies?'

'Well, you know. It's not our area anymore Charlie, but there are so many of these refugees now, the boats are happening every day, twice a day sometimes, so I don't know…. here, I'll send you a contact I have…'

Charlie's attention waned as he noticed Becky had moved further up the promenade towards a man was being violently sick by the side of the road.

'Here, Jacks, I've got to go, but thank you. Yeah?'

'Yeah, no worries, young man. Always good to hear from you!'
'Likewise. Listen, I'll pop in for a coffee soon, yeah?'
'That would be great.'
A car pulled up alongside Becky and the man.
Two men got out.
Charlie put the phone down and walked quickly to catch up to his friend. She reminded him so much of himself when he was younger. Always running towards trouble, when everyone else was moving the opposite way.
'Ahmed! Feeling a bit peaky are you?' Johnny said as he shut the car door and put a cigarette into his mouth.
'Mr Mac! Mr Mac! This no good, Mr Mac!' the man said, keeled over, spit dripping from his lips.
'It's all right, just breathe and relax…' Becky said, rubbing Ahmed's back, trying to calm him.
'That's all right young lady, we can take this from here.' Art said.
'I hope you don't think he is coming in the back of my motor,' Johnny said calmly, lighting his cigarette, eyeing up the sick man.
'I never go with you, never again! I rather die!' Ahmed started, before Johnny hit him squarely in the gut.
'Leave it out, pal!' Charlie shouted.
'Pal? I ain't *your* pal, *pal.*' Johnny said, tugging on his cigarette.
Charlie ignored him and continued to help the man from the floor.
'He needs an ambulance, Becky.' Charlie whispered. 'Go up the road and call 999.'

Becky nodded and started walking.
'Don't even fucking think about it. We'll look after him.' Johnny said calmly.
'No, he's getting an ambulance.' Charlie said firmly, standing in between Becky and the smoking man.
'Here, don't I know you?' Johnny asked, coming closer towards Charlie. 'Steve, do you recognise this guy?'
Steve got out of the passenger seat and looked him up and down, shrugged and got back in the car.
'Yes, ambulance please…'
'Don't do that, sweetheart!' Johnny said, walking towards Becky. Charlie held his hand out and stopped Johnny in his tracks. 'Why are your grubby hands on my jacket?'
'Why don't you take it elsewhere, hey? We can sort this out, OK?' Charlie said, trying to ease the situation.
Johnny's steely eyes met Charlie's.
'Yes, Fisherman's Wharf, I think a man has overdosed. You need to be quick…'
'Fuck him, let's get moving Johnny, all right?' came the voice from the car.
Johnny pressed his nose up to Charlie's, 'I'm going to remember your face.' Johnny said, before backing away towards the waiting car.
'I'll remember that breath, jeez…' Charlie said, as the car sped back towards the Folkestone one-way system.

6

A wave of anger washed over Charlie. What may have happened to Becky, had he not agreed to meet her on the beach? He let the feeling subside and turned his attention to Ahmed, who was beginning to hyperventilate.

'Ahmed, right?' Charlie said, sitting down next to him. 'Take a deep breath, in through your nose. Like this, see? Then out, push it out, through your mouth. OK? And again, Ahmed. OK?' Charlie looked up the street for the ambulance that was yet to arrive.

'Did you tell them it was an emergency?' he asked Becky.

'Of course I bloody did!'

'All right…' he said, beginning to notice a crowd forming. 'Becky, come sit with him. Here, wipe his brow with this.' Charlie passed her a hankie; he had noticed Ahmed was covered in sweat.

'Guys, please move on, OK. It's OK, an ambulance is coming.' Charlie asserted.

'What's he had one too many do you reckon?' One lad snorted.

'I thought them Muslims aren't supposed to drink?'

'There's a lot they aint supposed to do. Don't stop 'em though!'

'Thanks, lads. He's just sick.' Charlie said as the men quickly got bored and moved on. Charlie turned and kneeled beside Ahmed.

'He's getting worse,' Becky said.

'Ah, it's fucking burning! Oh my god…!'

'Ahmed, what have you taken? Can you tell me?' Charlie asked.

'Not taken…' Ahmed was convulsing now, his whole

body shaking.
'What are we going to do, Charlie? He's going into shock!' Becky asked.
'Ahmed, what have they given you? You know those men, don't you?'
Ahmed nodded.
'Not just…aaahhhhh!' Ahmed wretched in pain as the ambulance swung around the corner, blue lights flashing. Becky ran to the corner and flagged it down. Just as the van pulled to a halt, two mopeds arrived, speeding around the corner, one lad on one and two on the other. The one on the back stopped by Ahmed and pulled out a small handgun, pointing it at the ambulance driver.
'Leave him,' he said through his helmet, the voice of a young man.
'Are you sure you know what you are doing?' Charlie said, walking slowly towards the lad.
'Don't be a fucking hero, old man.' The voice came again.
'Old! I'm only 40!'
The other two lads slung Ahmed on the back of the moped and he slumped onto the driver's back.
'Tie him.'
The youngster secured Ahmed's limp body to the frame of the bike and then once around the driver.
'Fucking step back, you old cunt.' The boy with the gun said once more to Charlie, who now was in his face, smiling at him.
'You don't intimidate me, *young* man.' Charlie said calmly.
'Oh fuck off,' the boy said smashing the butt of his pistol into Charlie's mouth, before speeding off with his cargo on the back.

'Charlie!' Becky shouted.
'It's nothing, just a bloody peashooter, relax,' he said.
'But you're bleeding!'
'Well looks like I'm back, doesn't it? And yes, we do have our first case.' He smiled at Becky.
'Yes!'
'Did you get any of the plate numbers?'
'No, Charlie. It was all a bit of a blur, but they went out of town up towards the East Cliff.'
Charlie spat some blood onto the street.
'Listen, let's leave this for today, yeah? I need to get to a meeting. Let's catch up tomorrow.' Charlie said.
'Sounds good... partner!' Becky said, smirking. On that note, Charlie passed her a wry smile, before walking back to his car.

He sat in the driver's seat and searched the local AA meetings.
His heart was racing; angry and confused.
When he was in this state of mind, he knew he needed support; otherwise he could sink deep down into the depths of despair that had become his home for most of his life.
Despite the world of pubs, bars and drinking being a comfort to him, he knew in his heart that it was a false economy. When he awoke tomorrow, bleary-eyed and heavy-headed, craving another drink, the spiral had begun.
He pulled into the community centre in Alkham and realized that he was five minutes late... not ideal. Charlie checked his appearance in the rear-view mirror and wiped away the excess blood onto his sleeve.

Not that his appearance mattered at the meetings, there was no judgment. He had seen guys come in in all sorts of states and it was OK. They were a community. They were there to support one another.
Charlie walked in quietly and grabbed a seat at the back of the room.
'… She was screaming at me to stop it, but I couldn't. I just couldn't stop crying. Crying and crying and crying…' came the voice.
Heads nodded in understanding.
'Welcome…' spoke another, the organiser, who was looking directly at Charlie. '… would you like to speak?'
Charlie sat down and immediately heard his phone go off in his pocket, which echoed loudly through the room.
'Sorry… let me turn that off. Good afternoon everyone. I'm Charlie, and I'm an alcoholic.'
'Welcome, Charlie,' the group added as a collective.
'I have been an alcoholic for twenty-five years…'
Collective nods and solemn looks from the rest of the group.
'I have been thinking recently about something that happened to me…' Charlie continued.
'Yes, Charlie…' the organiser added.
'I had a…'
The rest of the room waited.
'I um…'
The organiser nodded and smiled with encouragement.
'I had a breakdown. Like, I think it was caused by a lot of external factors to do with my job and how dangerous it was but…'
There was a sharp intake of breath from one of the

souls in the room.
'... Nevertheless, it was exacerbated by drinking excessively. I mean, I thought I could trust the pub and a pint for solace and an escape from the evils I had endured... I had seen, but...'
'Go on, Charlie...'
'... It just added to the paranoia and the madness and the feeling you are being swallowed whole by all of your problems. I had to create some other world where I could live, but then... that disappeared...'
'How are you getting on now, Charlie?'
Charlie broke out of his trance and regained his focus.
'Now? It's OK. It's safe and comfortable and I feel in control. It's a bit boring, if I'm honest...'
A few of the men snorted with laughter.
'... But I guess that's the price you pay...'
'Thank you, Charlie for sharing with us. Now, would anybody else like to speak?'
Charlie listened to a man who was homeless due to his drinking and drug use, but was beginning to get back on his feet thanks to the Salvation Army. Then he listened to a young woman who was addicted to Apple Sourz.
From the time she awoke up in the morning she craved it and was currently getting over a five bottle a day habit.
In the grand scheme of things, Charlie counted himself lucky.
He checked his phone in the interval and saw that it was Tara, ready for collection. He made his apologies to the organiser who was understanding and kind and reminded him to keep attending meetings.
He smiled and made his way from the building. As he

stepped outside into the cool night air, he felt lucky.
There were a number of times he could, and probably should have died in his life. He was scarred and battered, but he was still here and now he was a father again.
He felt a warmth inside of him.
As he got in the car and headed for the M20, he also wondered what on earth had happened to Ahmed?
Was he dead, did he survive?
Tomorrow, he would start doing some digging.

7

The warm sterility of the William Harvey Hospital hit Charlie as soon as he entered the building.
The air was thick with a mild scent of vomit and baby poo. Still, it did not affect his excellent mood and feeling of lightness that enveloped him.
He scampered as quickly as he could to the Folkestone Ward and pressed the buzzer.
The area was quiet, with few nurses around, so Charlie waited at the door.
After a few moments he pressed the buzzer again, twice.
He pushed the door, expecting to feel the weight of it against him, however it was unlocked, much to Charlie's surprise and slight trepidation.
He went in and up the bright corridor, to the reception area. It was unmanned as usual, so Charlie continued around to room three, bay C, where Tara had told him she would be.
He was greeted by the sounds of wailing babies and as he tentatively pulled back the curtain, he witnessed his wife holding their newborn as she slept silently.
Tara smiled up at him. 'Everything OK?'
'Yeah, not too bad.'
'What the hell happened to your face?' Tara said, reaching out towards him, as he recoiled away, remembering the lad on the moped earlier.
'Ah, yeah. A… um... slight disagreement with another motorist…'
'What, you are telling me this was road rage? It's not the nineties, Charlie!'
'Don't worry about it, I'm OK,' he said, trying to get her to relax. 'How are you feeling?'

‘Bored, really. Ready to get out of here. Just waiting for the nurses to bring me my prescription and then I can go.’

‘You could be waiting a long time, it’s like a ghost town out there. That might be why the door to the ward was left unlocked.’

‘What, really? The door to the ward?’

‘Yeah, it was really bizarre. The door was left ajar. I’m sure it just didn’t catch properly…’

‘You know, I have seen some weird things here, Charlie. At first I thought it was the painkillers, but I swear I keep seeing the same guy in here…’

‘Well, that’s not strange, hun, he’s probably a proud, new dad…’

‘No, that’s not what I mean… he’s like walking around with different babies… I know it sounds mad, but I’m sure that’s what I keep seeing.’

‘Perhaps, he’s a *nurse?*’

‘In a trendy new jacket?’

‘Hm, maybe not. Seems really odd.’ Charlie wondered how accurately his wife could see the faces of all the babies in the man’s arms and be certain that they were different babies that he was holding. I mean, *didn’t all babies look the same?* He thought to himself.

‘Then, I could have sworn I saw a nurse holding the babies as the mum’s went to the toilet and for a wash. Like picking up the babies and feeling them, checking their weight and stuff…’

‘It’s probably her job, babe! Stop overthinking things! Either way, I’ll be glad to get the hell out of here.’

‘Yeah, you’re probably right. Anyway, where is this nurse?’

‘I’ll go chase her up…’ Charlie said, getting up from

the bed.
'Don't be rude, all right? They are very busy!'
'As if…' Charlie smiled back.
He went out of the ward and back towards reception, where there was a little bell on the reception desk, which he rang twice to no avail. Along the corridor, a nurse bustled towards him, looking stressed and busy.
'Um, excuse me… ah…' but by the time Charlie had started talking, she was already around the corner and into the maternity ward. Charlie looked into the room and he could see that the doctor was doing the rounds with all of the patients; Tara would be seen and hopefully discharged at some point.
He saw her through the glass and indicated he was going to head outside for a walk. She nodded in agreement, pleased presumably not to have an impatient husband prowling around and making things more difficult.
Charlie turned on his heel and headed towards the main door. On the way out, he noticed a short, portly man with a black beanie hat on his head holding a baby. The man turned around and despite trying to keep his head down, managed to catch Charlie's eye. Charlie smiled and realised he recognised him from somewhere, where was it?
The man looked down and wrapped the baby up forcefully in a white blanket.
'Hey, how's it going mate?' Charlie said half in hope that the young man might recognise him.
The man carried on walking swiftly towards the main doors.
'Here, I'll grab those for you,' Charlie said, running after the man and pressing the silver button to unlock

them. Charlie got in front of the man and looked at his face again, as he did, the baby began to cry.
'Where do I know you from, pal?' Charlie asked.
'I have no idea who you are, I am afraid,' the man said leaving swiftly, with the crying baby held tightly in his arms.
'Hm,' Charlie wracked his brains and walked slowly around to the coffee shop, only to find it was shut this late at night.
His phone rang.
'Hi, I'm discharged, do you want to bring the car and meet me at the back of the hospital?' Tara asked.
'Sure thing,' Charlie said, putting the phone down and walking back to the car.
As he did, he remembered where he had seen the face before. It was the man driving the car earlier today, one of the McCarthy crew.
Charlie ran out into the car park, to see if any cars were leaving, but the night was silent. Now, what was a known gang member doing with a little baby in the middle of the night?

8

'Oh my god, look at her! *Look at her!*' Tara said, cooing and smiling over the little baby that was lying pride of place at the end of their bed.

'Are we going to take the moses basket off the bed?'

'Yes of course, but don't you just want to spend some time with her before we go to sleep?'

'Well, yeah, but…'

'Why don't you give her a cuddle?'

'Do you want an honest answer? I am still scared that I'll break her.' Charlie said.

'You can't *break* her, baby's are really robust you know.'

'She doesn't look that robust to me…'

'Give her a cuddle…'

'OK, but I am…'

'That's it, take her from me, hand under the bum and…'

'OK…'

'Charlie take her head, TAKE HER HEAD!'

'All right, why are you shouting? Jeez…'

'You have to be careful, she is very fragile…'

'I thought she was robust, a minute ago?' Charlie said smiling.

'You know what I mean! Smell her Charlie, *smell her…*'

'What..?' Charlie did as he was told and leaned into the baby.

'Hm, she smells of butter…' Tara said, before rolling over and closing her eyes.

The baby opened her eyes and stared at her father.

'My word, you are precious…' Charlie slurred, realising how tired he was. He lay the baby carefully

back into the basket and placed it by the side of the bed next to Tara.
'That's it. Good girl…' Tara said, half asleep.
It was a miraculous thing having a baby. No two ways about it, one of life's real, genuine miracles.
Charlie was overjoyed, although he didn't necessarily show it the way Tara wanted him too, with cooing and gushing.
But he had to be honest, he felt uncomfortable picking up his own baby when she was so small and so little. He was nervous about hurting her in any way and just wanted to take any risk out of the equation. Which made him wonder, what was that McCarthy guy doing in the middle of the night, rushing his baby out of the ward? Charlie presumed it was his baby, it had to be, surely?
Charlie made a note in his diary to check this out with Becky when they start their case tomorrow, but for now he turned off the light and placed his head on the pillow. He checked his phone for the time, 11.37pm.
The beauty of being sober is he knew that he would sleep a good seven hours solid until the morning. In fact, he slept very much like a baby.

Charlie awoke to screaming at 2.24am.
'What's going on?' Charlie turned on the light.
'It's Ridley, she won't take the boob…' Tara said sleepily.
'Ah, I see. Anything I can do?'
'Not really. Actually, can you get me a glass of water? I'm so dehydrated!'
'Sure…' Charlie went like a zombie downstairs to the kitchen and placed a clean glass under the cold tap. He gulped the first glass himself, before taking the

second one up to his wife.
By the time he had returned, both her and the baby were asleep. Charlie removed the little girl from her arms and placed her back in the cot again.

'Here Johnny, I think we may have a little problem...' Steve said down the phone, breathing heavily, a little panicked.
'Oh yeah? Well, why don't you just calm down a little bit and catch your breath first. OK?'
'I've just dropped the latest package with the wizard...'
'Oh, you mean 'your' wizard? The one you don't want me to know about? That one?'
'Johnny, it isn't like that. Please, he's just a... you know...'
'No I don't know, lil brother. Anyway, what's the problem?'
'I was in the hospital yesterday, and I saw the guy. The guy from earlier with Ahmed.'
'Right...'
'Well, he recognised me... he saw me with the package...'
'Did he? Well, that's not very careful is it?' Johnny said slowly.
'No, but what are the bloody odds? That a geezer we have had a run in with is having a baby at the exact same time as I am... you know...'
'I must admit, it is unlikely. Not impossible though, Steve. A little careless, if I may...'
'Thanks for that. What are we going to do about it?'
'Well, it's funny you should mention him, I have been doing a bit of digging about that fella. I know who he is now. Shamed super cop, Charlie Stone.

Remember?'
'What the guy who solved the Sunny Sands murder?'
'Yes, that guy... except now he is a recovering alcoholic, went a bit fucking doolally by all accounts... no job... difficult to trace... until now.'
'Looks to me like his bird's just had a baby. Perhaps I could find out a few things, eh?'
'Perhaps you could, little bro. Perhaps you could.'

9

The baby woke Tara and Charlie twice more, before the sun streamed through the blinds in their bedroom, and they decided to admit defeat.
Another of Charlie's real joys of sobriety was the morning. He woke up, thought about whether he drank alcohol the night before and gave a little internal whoop that he didn't. His head was clear and he was ready to get out of bed, headache and guilt-free.
Before that though, he rolled over and snuggled up to his wife, enjoying the warmth of her skin as she pushed back against him comfortingly. She smelt awesome and he felt grateful that he was alive and that he had this second chance to make it work with Tara.
'Hmph, I suppose we should get up...' Tara murmured.
'You stay, I'll take the baby downstairs,' Charlie whispered back.
'It's fine...'
'Listen, I know what I am doing. This is not my first rodeo, kiddo!' he said, the morning bringing a new found fatherly confidence.
'Yeah, but she will be hungry soon and unless there is something you are not telling me, you won't be able to feed her!'
'True!'
Charlie took the exchange as a sign that Tara was happy to look after the baby, so he got in the shower and started getting ready for the day. Once he was done, he joined his wife for a cup of coffee downstairs.

‘Hey, T, I think it’s time I started doing something you know…’
‘Oh, get back to work?'
'I mean, yeah…'
'That’s great, Charlie! I think you should. It will be good for you.’ Tara said a little too eagerly.
‘OK… I thought you would be a bit worried about it… you know, the danger and…’
‘Well, I think you need to be sensible, but I hope we are past all that now. And really, let's face it. The past is the past, so let's move forward from all of that.’ Tara smiled, taking a slug from her orange Le Creuset coffee mug.
This was a far cry from the Tara Stone that wouldn’t let him out of the house until he had recovered from his last episode. The Tara Stone who sorted out meds and doctor’s appointments and vetted his phone calls to make sure Jacko wasn’t luring him back into police work. Tara stared at the TV, unphased.
‘OK, I am going to head off then... to meet Becky,’ he said.
‘Oh, you guys are still going to work together on cases?’
‘Yeah… if that’s OK?’
‘Sure. I mean I still think I would make a better Robin to your Batman, but…’ she looked down at little Ridley, who was beginning to stir.
‘You know I’ll give you all of the juicy details, when I’m back anyway. Oh, and don’t forget, Maddie is coming down tonight.’ Charlie added. Maddie was Charlie’s twelve-year-old daughter from his previous marriage to Jo.
‘As if I would forget! Plus, it’s fajita Friday. I’ll get the bits if you like? Take Ridley out for her first trip

to Tesco's! Fancy that Ridley?' Tara said, before descending into a cacophony of goo-goo's and gaa-gaa's.
'Sure thing, T.' Charlie gave his wife a kiss goodbye and headed for the door, surprised how easy going she was being.
Not that she wasn't an easy going person, it just seemed that she had let him off the leash a little easier than he expected. Charlie had become a little used to the restraint that living together had provided.
It had protected him and kept him safe through some dark times, and now he felt a little strange with his new found freedom.
Charlie was reading a book entitled, *'How to be a great dad.'*
In it there was a section on how some women get a high for days after giving birth. Maybe that was it? Either way, Charlie was pleased that Tara seemed happy and content.
He checked the address for their new office space, The Workshop on Tontine Street and set off.

'I thought, Stone and Street Services, maybe?' Becky said.
'Sounds a bit like a knock-in shop!'
Becky cackled.
'Fair enough. How about The Charbex agency?' she tried. Charlie looked at her a little bemused.
'You know like, Charlie and Becky put together…'
'Oh I got it Bex… I just um…'
'Think it's rubbish, OK… let me think…'
'How about we concentrate on this case first, yeah?' Charlie suggested.
'Sure, but we can't have a business without a cool

name!'
'Yes, we can! Anyway, tell me what you know about these McCarthy brothers…' Charlie asked, sitting on a black chair, behind a black desk. 'By the way, I love the office space, I think we should sign up.'
'Yeah, it's great isn't it? Did you know there is a chute, like a flume that takes you from floor four to floor three? How awesome. Shall we say, six months?' Becky said smiling, knowing she was pushing it a little bit.
'Six months? Well… I do still have some of my redundancy money left so…. Go on then.' Charlie replied.
'Eek! Exciting, I'll email the lady and let her know!'
'Later, Bex! What about these McCarthy boys?'
'Right, yes. So… the McCarthy's have been a dodgy family in Folkestone for years. They own a number of properties, had a hand in the entertainment industry back in the day. The family also have… shall we say, some more illegitimate operations too. These have been passed to the two brothers, incidentally both twins, Steve and Johnny.'
'Hang on, twins?'
'That's right. But they're not identical as you might have noticed...'
'I see.'
'Well, the one who is a bit smaller and chubbier is known as 'Steve sausage fingers…'
'Becky, are you winding me up…' Becky snorted.
'I mean, it does sound silly, I know, but I'm telling you the gospel truth here.'
'Steve sausage fingers…'
'Yes, and his brother, who is taller, more slender, the guy you had a run in with the other day, is known as,

'Johnny piano fingers.''
'Right…'
'Although they are twins, you can tell that they are brothers, one has tiny little stubby hands and the other, well, I'm sure you can guess from the name…'
'How very odd. More odd that I have never heard of these guys.'
'I guess, but they have only really come up recently when you were… you know… anyway… until recently they have been small-time, running the drugs through the east side of town. They are sly too. Using kids to deal…'
'What like county lines?'
'Yep, exactly. They have a few houses. I know one of them is around Central. The kids start there, collect the phone and then do whatever they are told to do through the phone. They call it a burner as they throw it away if they get any hint of trouble from the authorities.'
'Yes, I have heard about this. Anyway, why do you think they are involved with the refugees?'
'No idea, this is what we need to find out. However, they are definitely intercepting the men as they come off the boats and taking them somewhere else. These men will usually have debts to pay for the travel, but not to the McCarthy's, that's settled before they travel. Which makes me wonder what on earth they want with them?'
'And what was happening with Ahmed yesterday? I mean, he was definitely on something, right?'
'Do you remember, he said he was 'given' something, rather than *taken* it. So, I wonder if that has something to do with it too.'
'Have you got a photo of these McCarthy brothers?'

‘Sure, have a look here.’ Becky googled a picture of the two men and Charlie immediately recognised the shorter one.
‘Here, this guy… he was in William Harvey Hospital last night... with a baby,’ Charlie said.
‘Wait, what..?’
‘Yeah, I tried to speak with him, but before I could, he disappeared.’
‘Are you sure?’
‘Absolutely, one hundred percent. It was this guy.’
‘The word on the street is that he is gay. Apparently, Johnny isn’t too happy about it, brought up with his dad’s old-fashioned ideology. Never had a girlfriend, let alone a wife, or a baby. So that is strange.’
‘Right, we need to find out a bit more about these boys. Where shall we start looking?’
‘We need to be careful, after yesterday they will have their back up. These days it’s not often you see them in public. They usually have their lackeys, or kids on mopeds doing their dirty work for them.’
‘That might be a good place to start then, eh?’
‘Yeah, let's take a little drive out to where the trap house used to be.’ Becky said heading for the door.
They took Becky’s small purple Ford Fiesta, as it was less likely to gain attention. Becky drove.
‘It used to be in Central Folkestone just off Radnor Park, if I remember…’
‘How do you know about it?’
‘Misspent youth, Charlie,’ Becky said, avoiding his look. He stared at the side of her face though as she pulled away.
‘My little brother got into some stuff a little while back. Nothing to worry about.’
‘Right.’

'Don't worry about Kyle. He is… what he is.'
Charlie knew better than to pry. He cared about Becky, but if she wanted to tell him more, she would do it in her own time.
'It's lunchtime so a bit early. They might be beginning to get their stock ready for later… maybe…' Becky continued.
'Radnor Park is a bit…you know… upmarket for organised crime wouldn't you say?'
'Yeah, but these things have moved on. It's all about hiding in plain sight. Vulnerable kids, BMX's, nice areas. Helps with the low profile.'
'I see.'
'Anyway, it's just up here.'
Becky turned the corner onto Brockman Road and brought the car to a halt.
'You see that one there, with all the windows blacked?'
'Subtle.'
'Yeah. Let's see if anyone comes in or out.'
'Or, lets knock? See what we can find.'
'Charlie, but that will blow our cover!'
'Yeah, but who are we? Just some concerned citizens from the other night. They don't know who we are…'
'Just give it a minute, Charlie.' Becky said, trying to assert herself.
It was a peculiar dynamic.
Of course, Charlie had the experience and the expertise, but Becky understood the streets and she had a knowledge of what life was like in Folkestone's murky underworld in 2022.
'I want to go and say hello,' Charlie said, undoing his seatbelt.

'Charlie, just sit tight would you?' Becky put her hand on his leg to stop him. 'These might be just kids to you, Charlie. But they are dangerous and fearless. I mean, one of them pistol-whipped you yesterday!'
'Ah, it was just a scratch…'
Just trust me OK, these gangs don't care, all right? The gang members pick them up, then train them up. They are like violent criminals, but without the fear that adults hold. We need to be careful.'
It wasn't in Charlie's nature to back away from the danger, but recent events had taught him a different way of doing things. From being carved within an inch of his life, and losing everything, he had to acknowledge that sometimes he didn't know best. In addition, he respected Becky and trusted her opinion.
'Fair enough, Bex.' He said, sitting back in the seat.
'Here, look at these two on the corner.'
Becky pointed up towards two young boys on BMX's on the corner of Radnor Park.
'They are just kids messing about…' Charlie started, but Becky shot him a glance.
'Watch,' she said as she slowly pulled the car closer to the two lads. They were both dressed in black and had hoodies over their heads. They were laughing and joking with one another, until one of their phones rang.
One of the lads answered and then they were off in two different directions.
'Which one to follow?' Charlie said.
'Let's go with the one who answered the phone, eh?'
'Good idea.'
The lad sped off along the pavement past the Park Inn, now boarded up, around past the train station and the Co-op, heading towards town. He turned down a

one-way street which made it difficult for Becky to navigate, but she managed to predict where he would go and came out near where he did around the back of Sainsbury's.

'I'm going to follow on foot.' Charlie said, getting out of the car.

He walked along Cheriton Place, where Junction 13 used to be, before watching the boy speed around the corner, past the Halifax and towards the Arch. Charlie ran after him, just in time to see the young lad walk into McDonalds and order himself a Double Cheeseburger from the Saver Menu.

Charlie followed him in and ordered two coffees from the flat screen ordering system, before coming out of the side door to find Becky. As he left, the young lad winked at him and smiled, before heading back to his bicycle.

'He must have known we were tailing him.'

'But how?'

'Unsure, Charlie. But it's a brave new world out there. Phone, text and social media connect these little fuckers. They are difficult to pin down.'

'So it would seem.' Charlie paused. 'Hang on, I've got a plan. Let's head down to the harbour. Park in the Burstin.'

'Oh, you do know how to treat a lady, Charlie.' Becky joked.

She pulled the car into the car park and then followed Charlie into the main reception and through into the bar.

'It looks quite like we can't beat them, so let's join them, eh? Two diet cokes please.' Charlie said as the barman sauntered around to take their order.

'I'll have leaded, please,' Becky stated.

'What?' the barman looked confused.
'One diet, one regular,' she confirmed.
'Right,' the barman said, sloping away.
'So, if we can't really tail them, and even if we do, we are just going to get led to someone trying to score, let's try and get some gear ourselves. Bring them to us.' Charlie said enthusiastically.
'Right, and then what?'
'Well... then... uhm... we can... I don't know, we will think of something I'm sure. Now talk to your brother Kyle, and let's get the number for one of these 'burner' phones.'
'You want me to ask my brother to score?'
'No, just to get us the number. You got any better ideas?'
Becky mulled over the proposition, before taking a large swig of her coke.
'Give me five minutes.'
Becky headed outside to the foyer of the Burstin and Charlie watched as she made her way across the front of the large window and into the car park. She was a petite girl height-wise, around five foot five inches, Charlie would guess. She was also well built in the sense that she wasn't slight, but she wasn't what some men would consider large either. Maybe what his mother would call 'big-boned' in the eighties, which Charlie always believed was a kind way of saying fat. It wasn't fat though, she was just... well built, perfectly in proportion. Of course, he was biased as she was his friend and Charlie wasn't blessed with many of those these days.
A thought flashed across his mind, as these thoughts tend to do, whether he could see himself with her. He tried very quickly to remove that thought from his

mind. As she stood there though, working hard, taking risks, saving lives potentially, her hair blowing in the wind, he couldn't help but feel slightly attracted to her.

Sort it out, Charlie. You've just had a baby! His inner voice said. *Well, it was you who thought about her in that way,* he retorted.

He remembered the words of his old mentor, Dave Woodward, 'if you can conquer the mind, Charlie, you can conquer everything life throws at you.'

Charlie definitely needed to continue working on this, as he really had some way to go.

'Sorry Tara, sorry Dave,' he whispered to himself before Becky returned to him.

'How did it go?' Charlie asked her.

'Got the number. He is curious, Charlie. Obviously.'

'What did you tell him?'

'I said that I had a friend who wanted to score for her birthday. I don't like lying. Especially to my family,' Becky said a little sulkily.

'Come on, kiddo. It's for the greater good. You know that.'

'Are you going to make the call, or do you want me to do that too?' she continued.

'Give us the number.'

Charlie took it and tapped it into the phone. Becky watched on.

'No, don't try and withhold your number, they wont answer...'

'Really?'

'Yeah, well they have to be careful too that you know, they are not being... setup...'

'Indeed...' Charlie tapped the number in again and dialled. Waited.

'Yeah,' came the gruff voice on the other end of the line. It certainly didn't sound like a child to Charlie.
'Yeah, hi. I got this number from a pal... I wondered if I could pick up...'
'What you want?'
'Erm, just two...'
'Where are you?'
'Burstin, but can meet you somewhere...'
'Car park... five minutes.'
The line went dead.
'Wow, what a simple service!' Charlie mused.
'They will be there on time too. Do you know what you are buying?' Becky smirked.
'Ah, good point... no... not really...'
'Right, I think you have bought two wraps of coke. That's going to be eighty or a hundred pounds...'
'What? Are you kidding me?'
'Fraid not. Times have changed since you were a teenager, hey Charlie?'
'I'll say. I guess we will have to put it through expenses, eh?'
'Whatever, but chop chop, there is a cash machine over there in the corner.'
Charlie got the cash and paid the £1.95 fee that the machine charged him, before returning to Becky.
'OK, I'll go out and do the deal, you stay in the car and be ready to follow him. I'll catch you up afterwards.'
'OK, but be careful, all right?'
'What are you worried about, I've dealt with far bigger things than this...'
'Yeah, maybe. But you have always been protected by the badge before. Now you're just some guy picking up some gear in the Burstin car park.' Becky

stated, more out of concern than anything else.
'Well, cheers for that Bex. See you a bit later.'
He went through reception and around the side of the building, looking for any lads wearing black. He surveyed the scene for bikes or mopeds, but sadly, there was nothing. He stood and waited, shifting his feet from side to side. He checked his phone and had a message.
Chip shop over the road.
Charlie knew where they meant and looked for Becky who should have been in sight by now. He pondered texting her but then thought better of it. If he was being watched, maybe it wasn't such a good idea. He went towards the chip shop and looked around.
Inside there were three kids all shouting to one another as they waited for their fried food. *Maybe it was them*?
Charlie waited.
His phone buzzed again.
Corner, by the steps.
Again, he understood where the text meant and so he walked west towards the steps that climbed the cliff face, towards the Folkestone Arch.
A few cars came around the one-way system as he waited at the bottom of the steps.
He wondered where Becky had got to.
'Here,' a voice came from behind him. The voice was deep and had that estuary twang mixed with London mock gangster that seemed to be the new soundtrack to the Folkestone streets.
He turned around to see a young girl, possibly fourteen years old, in a large men's puffa jacket. She had long brown curly hair and despite her greasy skin and outwardly hostile approach, was a pretty, young

girl.
'Hundred, bruv.' She said, looking away and up the street.
Charlie fumbled in his wallet and eventually retrieved the wad of plastic notes.
'Right,' the girl checked the money and took it before passing Charlie two paper lottery tickets wrapped up in a perfect rectangle.
'Safe,' the girl said as she skipped back up the steps and out of sight.
Hm, not really. Charlie thought. Becky wouldn't be able to follow this girl as she was on foot. The car would need to make it all the way around the one-way system and she would lose them by the time she had done that.
Charlie waited a few moments, before following her.
He realised the absurdity and implications of a grown man following a teenage girl, but if he didn't, they would have literally no leads on how to get to the McCarthy's. As he got to the top of the steps, he noticed the girl talking to a teenage boy on a bike. She seemed to hand him the money, gave him a slobbery French kiss and he sped off down the hill on the bike. Just as he did, Charlie noticed Becky coming up the hill in the car. He stopped her and jumped in.
'Turn around at the roundabout.'
'Sure.'
Becky stayed at around twenty-miles an hour, slow enough to stay behind the kid, but also a good speed so as not to gain any unwanted attention.
The boy went around the harbour area past the George and Gillespie's and took a right up the hill and past the petrol station along Tram Road.

Becky kept a fair distance whilst keeping him in sight. At the top of the road, there was a small entrance to an abandoned factory. The boy stopped and got off the bike. He looked around and Becky stopped the car. The kid carried on walking up the dusty track to the large metal gates where a sign read Highfield Industrial Estate.
'I'm going on foot,' Charlie said, jumping out of the car.
Becky nodded before pulling over at the side of the road.
The kid knocked on the metal door and waited. After a few moments, a slot opened in the door, like a dystopian movie and someone on the other side checked his identity. The metal door creaked open and the kid slid inside.
Charlie went back to the car.
'What do you make of that then?' he asked, not quite sure what his own thoughts were.
'That has been an empty facility for years. Maybe they are just using it to avoid any unwanted attention.'
'Yeah, but it won't take long to gain attention if there are little toerags coming in and out all of the time.'
'Yeah, perhaps it's just a place where the dealers lay low.'
The two sat deflated.
'Hang on a minute, is that…' Becky looked out of the front window of the car, towards the large metal gates.
'What?' Charlie said, trying to follow her eyeline.
'That… the chimney pole it's pumping out… stuff…'
'Well, looks like it's more than just a hideout for the

local shotters.' Charlie checked his watch. 'We're going to have to come back to this, Bex. I have got to pick up Maddie.'
'No worries, I'll drop you back to your car and then start devising a plan.'
'Sounds like a good idea. Tomorrow night, all being well, we may be able to pick this up.'
'Awesome.'
'Oh, and I had a thought. What about B.S. Investigative Services?'
'Hm... yeah, I'll work on that too.' Becky said, smiling at Charlie.

10

Charlie had some spare time before he picked Maddie up from Ashford station, so he stopped at his favourite coffee shop, Harris and Hoole in Crooksfoot.

One addiction for another, that's what they say, isn't it? He mused.

Well, coffee isn't going to kill him or send him over the edge mentally. Plus, it's far easier to know when you have had enough with coffee. He has had a few caffeine 'overdoses,' got the shakes, felt very uneasy and knew that he had to put the black stuff down for a little while. Since then, he tried to limit himself to three large coffees a day, maybe four if he was treating himself.

He got his drink to go and headed towards the station. Maddie's train arrived at 5.08pm and he wanted to be there in time to head her off, so she wasn't waiting around. The station was teeming with cars and commuters, kids in school uniforms, suited and booted bodies, itching to get home for some downtime.

Charlie waited in the parking area for his daughter to arrive and she did at 5.09pm. Not bad for Southeastern trains. He smiled at her as she bustled towards the car with her school bag on her shoulders and long hair blowing in the wind.

She had really grown up into a fine young girl, he thought proudly.

'Hey, dad!' she said, opening the door.

'Hi, Mad. How was the journey?'

'Busy! I had to stand most of the way.'

'Oh, that's a shame,' Charlie said sensitively,

although secretly he liked Maddie on busy trains, as he knew it was generally safer for her.
They headed home via the supermarket. It was fajita Friday and it was always a bit of a ritual to get the food together and then cook it together. Maddie also enjoyed picking the chocolates for dad's pick n' mix, which consisted of about six chocolate bars all chopped up into bowls for the three of them. T had probably got the ingredients when she went to Tesco's earlier, but there was no harm in having too much food, right?
'Hey, dad, did you manage to get the ticket for football tomorrow?'
'No, no. I couldn't really… sorry…'
'Oh, right, OK.'
'Yeah, you're going to have to stay with Tara and the new baby, while I head up and watch West Ham take on our biggest rivals…'
Maddie looked up at her father dejectedly.
'Of course you have a ticket for tomorrow!'
'*Yes!* Thanks dad!'
'Spurs at home, you're not missing that one.'
'I can't wait!'

The evening passed without incident.
Maddie and Charlie cooked while Tara watched TV. Maddie held the baby tentatively, but like her father, was quite happy to give her back for fear of doing something wrong!
At around 9.30pm, they went up to bed and did the crossword puzzle together, before Tara got too tired and kicked Maddie out of the master bedroom. Gone were the days of tucking her in and reading her a story sadly. It was now iTunes and YouTube before

light out at 10pm.
Saturday came around all too soon, with Ridley waking her parents up at 5.24am.
Charlie got up and went for a short run, half an hour around the block and up to the McArthur Glen Designer Outlet.
By the time he had got back and showered, Maddie was up and ready for a day out in London.
'What do you reckon then today, dad?' Maddie asked.
'I'm too nervous to even guess what's going to happen!' Charlie returned.
'I know! Hopefully everyone is fit…'
'Yeah, I think so. Except maybe Coufal…'
'That's OK, we have Johnson.' Maddie said, smiling.
Charlie marvelled at how this young girl had embraced his football team with such fervour. A wave of pride engulfed him as they said their goodbyes and headed towards the station.
When they arrived, there was seven minutes until the train arrived. The queue at Costa was long, so they decided to play it safe and go straight to the platform. The train was already there so they went to the front, which was usually emptier, and boarded.
There were a number of West Ham shirts and nervous faces already on the train. No-one enjoyed the Spurs game. The thought of losing to them, at our stadium, was unthinkable. It was simple being a West Ham fan. Play well, beat Spurs and Millwall and anything else was a bonus. That was the west ham way.
Spurs' fans had a habit of being very vocal and vociferous if they won, yet disappear off the face of the planet when they lost. As it happened, Charlie had not seen one Tottenham shirt yet, but it was early in

the day.
'Someone on the TV earlier said that West Ham were actually favourites today,' Maddie said.
'Yes, we are. Feels weird. But they rested their whole team, all eleven of them in their midweek European game. We rested six,' Charlie added.
'Yeah, and they lost, didn't they? And we won!'
'Exactly that, Maddie.'
'Yeah, I'm not happy that their players will all be fresh…'
'Don't worry about that. It's more important that you win and keep winning and we have won two in a row now…'
Maddie smiled and looked out of the window. The train was meant to depart a few minutes ago, and it was unlike the fast train to ever be late.
The crackle and fuzz of the driver tannoy pricked Charlie's attention.
`Good morning all, We are sorry to announce that the train will terminate here due to a lack of trained staff available for the journey. All alight at Ashford.'
There was a collective groan from the passengers who heaved themselves from their seats.
'Looks like we will have time for the Costa after all!' Charlie said.
They walked back to the main part of the station where they got in line for drinks. Charlie ordered a black coffee, while Maddie had a decaf coffee frostino.
They mulled over sitting in Costa, but the next train to London was only twenty minutes away, and of course it would be busy.
'Let's head back to the platform, dad.' Maddie said, erring on the side of caution as he had often taught

her to do.
The second train left on time and rattled through the glorious Kentish countryside towards Stratford International. Once there, Charlie agreed to meet his friend, Don, at the Holiday Inn. Charlie preferred it at the hotel bar, as it was a slightly more sedate place to have a drink before the match. The down side was the extortionate prices, but Charlie was happy to stomach that for just one or two.
He ordered his pal a pint of Birra Morretti, while Charle and Maddie stuck to the Coke Zero's.
'I have always wanted to cut back on my drinking…' Charlie's friend said, in relation to Charlie's recent sobriety. 'It's just hard…'
Charlie laughed, 'yeah, you could say that. Especially given how much we used to drink at university.'
'But also you know… being single, and 40, how do you socialise with other men, without the pub?'
Charlie nodded sagely. 'It's virtually impossible…'
'I mean, you could meet in the pub and try not to drink, but then everyone else will be. What happens if your mates buy you a drink? Do you just say no, I'm not drinking? Or do you have one?'
'One!'
'Exactly, it's never one is it? And then you might as well have not bothered.'
'This is why it's easier for me to just not go out. Boring, I know, but if I am with the family and not out and about, I avoid the temptations…'
'Yeah, but I don't have 'the' family, Char.'
'I know mate. It's uh… it's difficult. I guess, if it's bothering you, just try and moderate as best you can, maybe?'
'Yeah, it never seems to work though!'

Charlie sympathised with his friend who vocalised the angst of Generation X. Raised to drink like fish and unable to escape the net. Charlie pondered if he didn't have the security of his family, would he be able to maintain sobriety? He wasn't sure he liked the answer.

'Right, we've only got half an hour, best get on our toes!' Charlie said, getting to his feet.

They took a swift walk to the London Stadium, passing the stragglers in The Cow, the touts hocking tickets and the street sellers with their half-and-half scarves.

Security was quick for a change, but the queues for the turnstiles were long. Luckily, there were security guards on the gate, who helped the queue move along and after a wee each, Charlie and Maddie were at their seats a few minutes before kick-off.

The game was a tense and edgy affair, Charlie on tenterhooks for the duration.

In the second half, after the game looked destined for a nil-nil draw, a corner came in from Aaron Cresswell, that somehow evaded two Tottenham defenders and landed at the foot of West Ham striker Michail Antonio, who poked it in, much to the chagrin of his opposite number Harry Kane, who was supposed to be marking him.

Charlie, whose seat was at the other end of the large ground, noticed the arms of the fans raise aloft in unison, as the ball hit the back of the net. Then the noise erupted into a cacophony of raucous yells of joy. Maddie grabbed her dad and there they were, a glorious moment, awash with delirium.

The game ended 1-0, triggering the soundtrack for the afternoon 'Tottenham get battered everywhere they go!' It was sung in the stadium, as fans left the stadium, on the trains, tubes, streets and supermarkets of East London. The atmosphere was nothing short of carnival-esque. Of course, Tottenham didn't really get battered, but why let the truth get in the way of a good yarn, eh?

Tara and Charlie didn't have a door knocker, or indeed a bell, so the sound of the heavy metal letter box, clanking twice, jolted Tara from her afternoon nap.

She looked out of the front room window to see a man in a high-visibility jacket standing just inside the porch. She sighed, checked that Ridley was OK, and raised herself to the door.

She still felt very achy and sore from labour. Her body was heavy, filled with fluid and she felt disgusting. Checking her appearance in the mirror, she didn't look much better in her opinion. Her hair was straggly and her face red and puffy.

She opened the door to a tall, slim man with a clipboard in his hand. He smiled. She noticed that he was handsome in an east-end cockney kind of way. His hair was combed to the side and his bright blue eyes piercing, as she stood half asleep in the doorway.

'Tara? Tara Stone..?' The man asked, looking down at his clipboard.

She rubbed her eyes and yawned.

'Haven't caught you at a bad time, have I?' the man's eyes darted around the inside of the house.

'Who are you?' she asked, noticing his long, spindly fingers.

'You don't know me…' the man said, placing his clipboard by a pile of shoes on the porch before

grabbing Tara by the crotch and thrusting her against the hallway wall.
She went to yelp, but those long fingers wrapped themselves tightly across her mouth.
'Don't be scared,' the man said, easing inside the house and shutting the front door behind him with his foot.
Tara breathed heavily and tried to bite the man's fingers to free herself.
'Don't try that sweetheart,' he said, thrusting his hand and fingers harder and deeper into her groin. Tears formed in her eyes.
'Now, you don't know me, but your old man does…' Johnny continued, pushing himself further onto her, his warm breath and spit collecting in her hair.
She wailed and he pushed harder up against her. Johnny was aroused, and breathing heavily, his fingers pushing harder into her.
'We are going to send dear Charlie a little message…' he snarled, all teeth and saliva, centimetres from Tara's face.
She wept, forlorn.
Then the sound of the baby stirring, and crying, caught their attention.
Johnny immediately removed his hand and let Tara go. He looked down at his hand that was now flecked with blood from where she was healing from childbirth.
'Fucking disgusting!' He shouted in her face, before grabbing her shoulders and smashing her head hard against the hallway wall.
Johnny re-opened the front door and snuck out as Tara's body fell into a ball on the floor.

11

'What time did they say they were delivering food, dad?' Maddie asked as they skipped up Hythe Road, full of joy.
'Should be there anytime. Hopefully T will grab it, if we are not back yet.'
'Oh good, I'm starving!'
'Hang on a minute, you have had a bag of crisps and a packet of Revels on the train. Plus you had a pie at the stadium, and you are *still* hungry?'
'What can I say, dad… growing girl, aren't I?'
'I guess so! Anyway, won't be long until we are back. Fancy stopping in at the pub and watch a bit of the Man U v Liverpool game?' Charlie asked.
'Could do.' Maddie answered. Charlie could tell she just wanted to get back for her Chinese dinner though.
As they walked past the pub, Charlie looked in.
'Looks a bit busy, eh, Mad?'
'Yeah, let's go and see T and Ridley.'
Charlie smiled and nodded.
His key entered the door and he could sense that something was wrong. The house was quiet and T was nowhere to be seen.
'T?' Charlie shouted, looking in the downstairs rooms. 'T!'
Charlie sprinted up the stairs to find baby Ridley lying on the bed sleeping. He checked the bathroom where he found T laying under the water in the bath.
Charlie panicked and shook her. She jumped up, spraying water everywhere and shouting at him from underneath the surface.
'What's the matter? It's only me.' Charlie said softly.

He could tell she had been crying. Her hands were shaking.

As he went to hug her, she pulled him in close and began crying again.

'T, talk to me. What's happened? Is something wrong with the baby?'

Tara was crying so hard that Charlie took control of the situation and pulled her out of the bath, wrapping a towel around her and placing her onto the bed. Maddie was at the top of the stairs, staring at the scene, a little in disbelief.

'Mad, get your pyjamas on, yeah?' Charlie said. She nodded, going into her bedroom and closing the door behind her.

Tara had calmed a little as she sat up on the edge of the bed.

'What's going on?' Charlie said, a little more forcefully.

'S… s… something… happened this afternoon…' Tara began. Charlie took a deep breath and steeled himself for what was to come.

12

Charlie was back in the rooms, talking. He felt waves of anger, sadness, nausea.

'It was my boss, my uhm... best friend, I guess. It's difficult when you are in the force for so long, doing what we did. You don't want to go and socialise and be pally, and drink wine and play board games of a weekend.

You wanted to hide away. You wanted to protect your own. You just wanted to sit and drink away the horrors that you had seen, the evil you had encountered, the pain you had caused.

That's how I felt anyway.

And it all started going wrong for me when he died. When Dave died. He followed me because they had my daughter, they took her. I can't say where, but...

She was in very serious danger and so I ran in, without thinking and... he followed, like a true friend.

But he was too old, he didn't have my speed and he got caught, injured... hit with this poison that, if I had known, if I had thought to ask, I could have saved him, but I was too centred on my own problems, too focused on that rather than him and so I...'

'Charlie, this is all your fault...' the therapist said.

'Wait, what?'

The lady laughed. 'You heard me, it's all your fault.'

'But, I never meant to...'

'Come on, you know as well as I do, all of that bullshit about it not being you, it's circumstance, he died doing what he would have wanted, is all a crock...'

'But, what about the Mustang?'

'Fuck the Mustang! It's your fault!'
'Yes, yes, it's my fault, it's my fault, it's... my...'

Charlie came too. He was driving along the motorway, towards Folkestone. He took a deep breath and steeled himself, trying to remove the duvet of guilt that had wrapped around him.
Maddie wasn't there, then he remembered he left, as calmly as he could so as not to arouse any suspicion amongst the girls, that he was going to do something crazy.
He checked his phone, he had two messages, one from Maddie, one from Becky. He connected to Bluetooth and threw the phone back on the passenger seat.
'Hey, Charlie. How long?'
'Ten minutes. Have you got anything?'
'Not really since yesterday.'
'Well, it looks like tonight is the night, we need to go in under cover of darkness, see what we can find.'
'Sure thing, boss.'
'These McCarthy's... one of them visited my house.'
'Wait, what?'
'Exactly. Manhandled Tara, threw her against the wall. Trying to shake me up. Shook her up, all right.'
'Which one?'
'The big one, thinks he's Reggie Kray.'
'If only. You could reason with him at least. Jesus Christ, Charlie. Do you not want to be with her?'
'I have been. Plus, Maddie is there, the door is double locked and the CCTV is on. They are eating Chinese food and watching Friends. They're safe.'
'OK, OK...'
'So, where do I find this guy?'

'Charlie…'
'Trust me, I need to find him.'
'Charlie, firstly you can't just *find* him. They have a number of different hideouts and houses that they use. But also, you can't just go up to him and arrest him…'
'Oh really?'
'Yes, really! These guys are serious, Charlie. That's a warning, probably for the other night. You need to box clever with this one.'
'Hm. We need to sort him though, Becky.'
'Oh, we will. But a good place to start is this factory and what is going on there. Meet me at the top of Dover Road, I have a plan.'
Becky ended the call as Charlie put his foot down and drove the final stretch towards East Folkestone.
Charlie reached Wear Bay Road and pulled the car to the side of the street. He checked his phone again and read the previous text by Becky and then the new one.
Are we working tonight?
I am by the pearly whites. The two texts read.
Charlie was a little bemused by the cryptic nature of the second text, so opened the one from Maddie.
Don't worry dad. I will look after T. Love you xxx
He initially felt a pang of guilt that he had left her alone. However, given a moment to reflect on what she had sent, he realised that she was genuine. She just wanted to support her family.
Charlie smiled.
Like a lightbulb moment, Charlie understood the text from Becky. She meant the Arm and Hammer factory that sits nestled amongst the suburban homes upon the East Cliff. She must be there. Charlie left the car,

locked it and walked towards the destination.
Lo and behold, Becky was there wearing a black Beanie and a skintight black top that revealed her feminine attributes a little more than Charlie had expected. The combo was finished off with black jeans, and… you guessed it… a pair of black Timberland boots.
'Well, hi!' Charlie said smiling.
'What, Charlie? You got something to say?'
'I just… want you to be careful, that's all. You could take someone's eye out with one of those,' Charlie said, nodding towards Becky's chest.
Becky gave him a sideways glance.
'You do realise that this is the era of women's lib, Charlie. Have you heard of the Me Too movement?' she said half-jokingly.
'Yes, of course dear. However, I am stuck very much in the eighties, I am afraid. Oh, and on that note, the Milk Tray man called and asked for his outfit back…'
'Oh fuck off, Charlie. I thought I looked pretty…'
'Pretty?'
'Not like that! Pretty… *professional?*'
'Yes, that could be your new nickname, pretty professional. As opposed to me, pretty bloody useless.'
'Oh, bless you. You're not that bad old man. Anyway, about the job. This factory closes in five minutes. Once all of the workers have cleared out, I reckon we can get a direct line from the back end of the factory into the back of the McCarthy place. Look…'
Becky showed him a copy of Google Maps, but to be honest, it was all a bit too much prep for Charlie Stone. He knew, as the crow flies, that the place he

wanted to scope out was about four hundred metres due South East and that was the way he was headed, regardless of what was in the way.
'Sure, great work, Catwoman…' Charlie said.
'Charlie, just because you are jealous of my outfit, you don't have to keep going on about it…'
'No, you are right, you look the part, no more sneidy jokes I promise. Scout's honour.'
'As if you were in the scouts! You would have had to follow instructions, no chance!'
'Miaow!'
'We can call that evens. Anyway, let's get moving.'
'But didn't you say that it was kick out time? Won't the workers be coming out now?'
'It's a good thing I am here, eh? It's one way Charlie, they all funnel out onto Dover Road, halfway up. We're clear.'
'Of course. Just testing, I knew that. Promise.'
The pair continued towards the facility that was now aglow with fluorescent factory lighting. The sun dipped and the strange glow of dusk kept them out of sight, despite there being nobody around at this time.
'If we head through the car park, there should be a way we can scale the wall at the back.' Becky whispered.
Charlie nodded, following his partner as she navigated through the gloom and towards the end of the concrete car park.
At the end of it, there was a large brick wall, too tall to scale and atop there was barbed wire and glass shards cemented into the peak of it.
'Hm. Someone does not want us to get in.' Becky mused.
'That's OK. When in doubt, take the road less

travelled…'
Charlie disappeared towards the side of the building and across to the west of the site. There were a few garages dotted along the western wall.
'Here, fancy a bunk up?' he said.
'You really are a product of the eighties aren't you? But since you ask, yes. Good idea.'
Charlie placed his hands ready for Becky's weight. She stepped in and pulled herself up to the top of the garage with relative ease.
'Here,' she said, reaching her arm down to help lift him up.
'Don't worry about me, there is an old chair over here, I'll use that,' Charlie said, skipping off to grab the old velour carcass that was once the pride of place in someone's home.
'Oh, cheers for telling me about that!' Becky said.
'All part of the plan, I wanted to see if you could get yourself up there.'
'Bloody cheek! I am fitter than you, that's for sure, Grandad!'
Charlie shot her a glance and smiled.
'We will see about that.' He said, slightly hurt, but putting a brave face on it.
He stood on the old chair and pulled himself on top of the garage, before surveying the surroundings.
'Right, if we jump into that field, we will have more luck getting in from the back of these houses and …. what are they? Commercial premises…from this side? What do you think?'
'Sounds good to me.' Becky agreed, already jumping down and into what appeared to be a derelict field filled with wooden pallets.
Charlie followed. Currently, they were about a

hundred metres from the north-west corner of the factory. They moved together towards the corner, to see if there would be a simple way to gain access.
'Look, no barbed wire on this side,' Charlie said.
'Yeah, but it's totally overgrown, there is no way we can get through…' Becky said, looking directly at the towering wall, covered in branches.
'The road less travelled, Bex.' Charlie said, looking directly down at a manhole cover below him.
'Oh, God no,' Becky said.
'It's the only way forward that I can see.'
Becky swallowed hard and fought back the urge to tell Charlie where to go. She knew that if she wanted to be taken seriously, she would have to get her hands dirty, quite literally. She thought about the new Timberland boots she had treated herself to this morning, and wept a silent tear for what may become of them.
In a few minutes, Charlie had undone the manhole cover and slipped himself inside. Becky tried to watch him, but in the dark and gloom, could see very little.
'Come on down! You'll love it in here!' Charlie said.
Becky took a deep breath and followed behind.

13

'Why do you love babies so much, do you reckon?' Johnny said, whilst swirling a half-eaten chicken bone around his mouth.

Steve looked at him blankly.

'Why don't you like babies at all?'

'Now, now dearest brother. You know why I don't like the little fucking blighters. We have been through this. And anyway, didn't mother tell you not to answer a question with a question?'

'Hm.'

'So?'

'So what?'

'So, why do you love babies?'

'For fuck's sake, it's not that I love them, it's just that… well, they are helpless and so, you know, it's nice to look out for them…'

Johnny sniggered. 'Oh right, and that's what you are doing is it? *Looking out for them?'*

'Can we drop it? It's business.'

'OK, OK. Let's change the subject. If you go in via the back way then Ron can cover the door for me. There's a good lad.' Ron was driving and nodded without saying a word.

They pulled up in the dark car park at the bottom of Cheriton High Street. The two brothers waited in the car while Ron parked, got out and wrapped on the big black metal door, coloured dimly with a pink fluorescent light.

After a minute, an old lady appeared and motioned to the car for Johnny to enter.

Steve and Johnny bustled out quickly and headed into the building, Ron waited for a moment, checked that

no one was following, and came in behind them. The lady double locked the metal door behind them.
'Steve, good to see you. Johnny… Are you partaking today?'
'Of course I am.' Johnny announced.
'Erm, no.' The smaller of the two brothers said, sitting down in the foyer area, his eyes already moving towards the small portable TV in the corner of the room.
'Oh, really? I sometimes wonder whether you are quite right, you know? Babies? No birds? Are you a fucking iron, Stephen?'
Steve turned to his brother. 'Look at the TV.'
As he did, he became transfixed by a news story that had gathered momentum recently. It was about the English Defence League, and pro-refugee protesters coming together in clashes on Folkestone beach.
Johnny nodded, a big grin spreading across his face.
'Very good, little bro. Very good indeed.'
'Johnny, sorry, but are you here for your…'
'Usual service, usual lady, Pam. I am a man of wealth and taste, as Mick Jagger once said.'
'OK, it's just erm, last time…uh…'
'Yes… spit it out…'
'Jenna couldn't work for two weeks, so….'
'Oh, I see. You want more fucking money?'
'No, no! It's not about the money at all, just Jenna will see you, it's just we need you to go a bit…'
'Just take it a bit fucking easy on the poor girl. What is she? 21?' Steve interjected.
'Yes, 21…'
'Well, I can't promise that, Pam. I can't promise that at all. But I'll tell you what I'll do. I'll take my money and fuck off elsewhere. You ain't the only gaff in

town y'know…'
'No, no. It's fine, Johnny. Just please, can you… no bruises, no scars…'
'Like I said, I can't promise sweetheart…'
Pam was close to tears. After a moment she looked up at Johnny Piano Fingers.
'OK. She is through here.'
'Get comfortable lads!' Johnny said, nodding at Ron and his brother who had settled into the sofa.

'If I am right, we need to head about fifty metres in…. this direction to get into the building, right?' Charlie said, pointing trying to get a compass app to work on his phone, but realising that underground, he had no reception.
'I would say so. Can we do it quickly please?'
'Of course. This is obviously a slightly foolhardy plan, Bex, as God knows where we come out. But if I loosen the cover slowly, given it will be completely dark by then, we should be able to sneak a peek before jumping out.'
'Roger that, boss.'
'OK.'
The pair headed through the sewer and in the general direction that Charlie suggested. With only a small torch light from Becky's phone, it was mainly guesswork, but Charlie was lucky to have a generally good sense of direction.
Looking up, he saw the manhole cover he wanted to try. He put his ear up to the underside of it.
'What do you think?' Becky asked.
'Difficult to say, there is a whirring, like a motor or engine or something on the other side…'
'Keep going?'

‘Yeah, let's.’
They carried on through the sewer, the sound of scurrying beneath their feet, as they continued through the stench and filth.
‘I mean the sooner the better, Charlie, yeah?’
Charlie turned to see Becky looking flustered.
‘Don’t worry, just up here,’ he said. When he found the cover he went through the same process. ‘Seems quiet, let's give this one a go.’
He started undoing it and when he had it loose, he pushed it open a crack and tried to see out of it.
‘I can't see. Let me lift you up Bex, to get a view.’
‘Righto…’ Becky positioned herself underneath the manhole cover. Charlie grabbed her waist and lifted her off the ground. She pushed it open and peeked out of the top. She could see what looked like a vehicle, but apart from that it was quiet.
‘Push me up,’ Becky said.
‘Are you sure?’
‘Push me!’
Charlie trusted his partner and steeled himself before thrusting her frame up and through the hole in the ground. She grabbed the edge and pulled herself up to safety. The coldness of the air hit Charlie, as Becky leant her arm down and he used it to lever himself up and out.
They were in a small concrete courtyard, and there was an ambulance parked to the right of them.
They looked at each other bemused, before Charlie indicated to stick behind him.
He stayed low to the ground and Becky followed his lead. He moved towards an old wooden door that opened with a gentle push and led into a derelict building that was at the far end of the site.

‘Let’s head upstairs and see if we can get a better view of what we are dealing with here.’ Charlie said, heading towards the old, rickety staircase, in a building that was almost certainly riddled with asbestos and could crumble to the ground at any minute.
They got to the top of the building and realised it wasn’t really tall enough to get a view over the whole facility.
As Charlie pondered his next move, Becky moved to the window and thrust her elbow through the glass, smashing the pane. She held her top over her hand and cleared the rest of the shards away, before jumping out of the window and up towards the roof.
Charlie stood back and admired her in action, he could do little but follow her and after a few moments they were both sat on the roof of the building, looking down at the site from above.
‘Check that out…’ Becky said, pointing directly ahead.
‘Not just some hoodlum hideout, huh?’
Becky shook her head as they both took in the scale of what they could see. Beyond this building and the one in front, slightly larger but also empty, was a hive of fluorescent light and buzzing activity.
There were two cars parked, and another ambulance, this one had medical practitioners and men in white coats standing by it, talking. The fluorescent lights beat down on the men milling around, all carrying clipboards and looking like they were working on something rather… *official*.
The lads on bikes were lurking at the side of the scene quietly, seemingly minding their own business.
‘What is this place?’ Becky mused.

‘Not sure Becks, but we need to find out. What do you notice about the scene?’ Charlie said, a little patronisingly but Becky didn’t mind, she liked it when Charlie asked for her advice.
‘This seems like a medical facility… like the doctors, the ambulances… it seems like they are testing something… ’
‘I think you’re right, but testing what?’
‘Let’s go and find out, eh?’
Before Charlie had time to respond, Becky had started moving and slipped back through the window. She poked her head through, ‘are you coming or what?’
Charlie sniggered at her brassiness, but got to his feet and followed her back into the old building.

'What shall we do with dad's food?'
'Just pop it on the side, sweet. Although I am sure he wouldn't mind you having some if you wanted.'
'No, he has that weird crispy beef, no thank you!'
'Fair enough, shall we sit and watch something? I can comb your hair if you like?'
'Why don't I comb your hair, T? You would like that wouldn't you?'
'No, no it's fine, Mad, don't worry.'
'Let me comb your hair, you are green!'
'Say... *what?*'
'Nothing... I was just....'
'You said I was green, what do you mean?'
'I don't really... talk about it..?'
'Hang on, you have said I am green and then said you don't really want to talk about it?'
'Sometimes... I um... see things in colours, you know?'

Tara nodded, she did know.
'So, like when people are angry, I can just see that they are bright orange and red or if the cat is scared of the chickens or she has had a fight, I see yellow…'
'Wow Mad, you know what? That's amazing. Do you know what they call that?'
'I dont want to talk about it too much, but yeah it's called hum...sini....synesth....something.'
'Close! Synesthesia. Have you told your dad?'
'Ah, not yet but we can tell him, I just don't want all my school friends thinking I'm weird.'
'They won't, it's like a sixth sense, if anything they will love it!'
'Hmmm, I'm not so sure…'
'So you said, I'm green, what do you think that means, huh?'
'It means you should come and eat your food and let me do your hair!'
'Well... fair enough!'

As Charlie and Becky moved closer to the hubbub of activity, occasionally the buzz of generic sound was pierced with a deep male scream. Something primal, otherworldly.
Charlie found it rather unnerving, yet also he knew he had a duty to find out what was going on here.
He moved to the side of the large building just as the ambulance engine roared to a start and began creeping towards a pair of large gates that were being opened by a hoodie-clad lad.
These were different to the gates that opened out onto Tram Road. They were to the west of the site and led in and out of the facility through another industrial facility. As such this entrance was very much

concealed.
'We need something that we can take away from here, something to take to Jacko.'
'That's not going to be easy.'
'Let's see if we can get into that building...'
'Where the screams are coming from?'
'Exactly,' Charlie said. 'If we skirt the perimeter we should be able to get across without being seen.'
'OK and what if we are seen?'
'Make a run for it. Either the way we came or as fast as you can out of the main gates. They are unlocked, so just need a push.'
'OK.'
'Listen, Becky. It may be safer if I go alone.'
'Oh great, and what am I going to do?'
'Perhaps wait back where we were earlier? On top of that old building? You can keep an eye out for me and text me if there is something dangerous, maybe? I don't think we can both make it across there together…it's a little risky.'
'Right. I'll head back and wait for you. Don't mess about Charlie, be quick.'
'Five minutes, see you at the top.'
Becky turned and slowly, covertly, snuck back to the old building. Charlie watched as she got into position. He gave her the thumbs up, before turning and heading into the unknown ahead of him.

'Sometimes with dad, I see a lot of different colours…. And numbers…'
'Go on…'
'Well, like, he can be beautiful red and then dark green and then go black, *really quick* you know?'
'Yes, I do know. He's a complex man, your father.

But that's what makes him so… *special.*'
'Also, I know this sounds *really* crazy…'
'It doesn't sound crazy, Mad!'
'Well, OK. But sometimes, I can feel what he feels…'
'Like in your stomach? When he's sad?'
'I mean, yeah kinda… but more if he is in danger. I can tell. Do you remember the night at the football? My stomach was churning and it was blood red, black. I didn't really know then what the syna… sinna….'
'Synaesthesia…'
'…Yes, that was all about. So, I couldn't use it to help then, you know?'
'Is your dad in danger now?'
Maddie laughed, 'No not now. Dad's happy. He is doing what he wants to be doing. Orange.'

Charlie manoeuvred behind a crate of plastic boxes, all marked with the words, *Medical Supplies.*
The courtyard was empty now, the ambulance had left and there was a gang of four youths, to his right, smoking cigarettes and talking quietly.
The movements in this facility were unpredictable, it seemed that anyone could arrive or come out from a building at any given moment, so Charlie wanted to keep his wits about him.
He wanted to eliminate any concern for Becky, he couldn't bear to think about anything happening to her and was glad she was in a safe space, despite feeling as well that he had belittled her somewhat too. Charlie's destination was due north of this point, and the group of youths were between him and that point, just to the left. He thought he could get around them

by keeping behind the pallets and boxes that were dotted around and hopefully reach the facility unscathed, where the fluorescent light was pouring from.
As he moved closer, he realised that he was dangerously close to the gang of youths. He fancied his chances of subduing the boys, but that wasn't the plan. The plan was to be covert and remain in the darkness. He checked his pocket and found the Swiss army knife he had used to remove the manhole cover. He looked towards an isolated block of pallets, a few metres from the building, and he threw the knife in that direction.
There was a loud clank and it immediately gained the gang's attention.
'What was that bruv?'
'Like a cat innit?'
'Dat ain't no cat, fam!'
Rather than split up to limit their potential danger, the pack moved as one towards the pallets. *Amateurs*. This was Charlie's opportunity and as the lads were distracted, he moved swiftly towards the large glass door of the facility.
He tugged at it and it opened, making a loud clicking sound, that for a moment left him thinking he had been rumbled, but he managed to sneak through the door and into the relative safety of the building.
Charlie checked his surroundings and stayed low.
He immediately heard voices along the corridor, in a room to his right.
He listened in.
'The strain doesn't work, not these batches…'
'So that's CVX100…'
'C-V-X…. yes, that's the one. It seems it slows the

rate but doesn't eliminate it completely.'
'Have you got the new batch?'
'Arrives at 4am.'
The piercing scream rose through the facility again.
Silence.
'And him?'
There was a sigh. 'If he gets too much, you can kill him. There's more arriving everyday.'
'Thank God.' The other man returned.
'Listen, I'm knocking off now. There's not a great deal to do until the new batch, when I will come back. Maybe try and get some rest for now.'
Charlie realised that the man would be coming down the corridor to his location, so he threw himself on the cold floor and army crawled into the room on the left. He lay silently on the floor as the man walked past. He had a white doctor's coat, and looked like a medical professional.
What on earth were these doctors doing in a place like this?
Once the door slammed shut, there was no further discussion or noise from the room across the way, so Charlie got to his feet and started to survey his surroundings. The room he was in was an unused operating room. There was a bed to the side, but otherwise it was empty.
Charlie crept back to the corridor and slowly moved along it. He peeked inside the room and noticed a second man in a white coat swinging slowly on an office chair, facing the opposite direction.
Charlie entered the room quietly and grabbed the man from behind, choking him until he fell unconscious.
He looked around again and noticed that he overlooked an operating theatre that was visible

through the large panes of glass in front of him. There were different types of buttons and knobs, not that Charlie really knew what any of them did.

On a metal table towards the far end of the room, Charlie found a clipboard that had the names of men on it, followed by some letters and numbers. He grabbed the papers before moving back to the sleeping man slumped in the chair. Charlie took up his badge and read, 'Doctor Robert Smith,' East Kent Medical Partnership.

A real doctor?

Charlie left the room and continued investigating. At the end of the corridor to the right, there was another locked door. He went back to the sleeping doctor and found his security card in his inside jacket pocket. Charlie swiped it in the door and was immediately met by the piercing scream that had provided the intermittent soundtrack to the evening's events.

In each cell there was a man, naked, apart from a pair of white briefs, in various states of distress or discomfort. Each man was of middle-Eastern origin.

Charlie tried the security card on the cells, but it wouldn't work. Perhaps the supervisor who had just left, was the one with access to these men.

One of them looked up at Charlie, but as Charlie tried to intimate to him, the man looked straight through him, glassy-eyed, half dead.

Charlie thought it best to quit with at least some documents and some new information, so headed back out of the building. He checked on Doctor Smith once more, who seemed quite content in his slumber.

Charlie crept out of the door, making sure he let it close quietly. The youths were nowhere to be seen now, probably called away on some other 'job,' so

Charlie's journey to the meeting spot with Becky was relatively straightforward.
He made it back through the courtyard, towards the old building and inside it. He traversed the stairs and through the window, but he couldn't see his partner.
'Becky!' he whispered. *'Bex!'*
She wasn't there.
Charlie hauled himself up onto the roof. He looked across the site, over at the fluorescent lights, to the pallets and to where the young lads were standing earlier. Nothing.
Charlie checked his surroundings and looked to the floor.
There was something dark. He put his hand down to see what it was. Blood.

14

‘'Ere boss. There has been a problem.’ Ron said.
‘Well it will need to fucking wait!’
‘I think you want to hear it…’
There was the sound of a bed creaking and moaning under the weight of carnal activity.
‘Boss?’
‘What is it?’
‘There’s been a break in…’
The movement of the bed stopped.
‘Where?’
‘The facility… Dover Road…’
Silence.
Johnny appeared at the door of the room.
‘Who the fuck is it?’ he whispered to Ron, Steve appeared in the corridor too, having just been on the phone.
‘No-one. That’s the thing. Some bird. Sitting in one of the unused buildings, scoping the place out.’
‘A lookout, Johnny.’ Steve said. ‘Check this out.’
Johnny showed his brother a picture of Becky on his phone, tied up, her face flecked with blood.
Steve smiled and looked at his brother. Johnny nodded in agreement, they recognised this woman from their encounter the other night.
‘Well, well. This cunt just won't take a hint, will he? Let her go,’ Johnny said, going back into the room and closing the door.
‘Are you sure?’ Ron asked.
‘Very. I’ll deal with Charlie big bollocks Stone later.’
The voices stopped and were replaced by the sound of a woman gasping, sobbing behind the bedroom door.

‘Now, now. Won't be long. And the best bit is yet to come!’ Johnny bellowed with laughter.

15

Charlie returned home, wrecked.

The girls were in bed, so he went through to Maddie's room and kissed her goodnight. Tara was awake, Ridley by her side.

'Hey,' she said.

'Hi.'

'How did it go? Any luck?'

'There is something strange. Dover Road. What looks like a derelict old factory... it's not.'

'Really, what's going on?'

'Some sort of medical testing facility.'

'Testing? Testing, what?'

'Humans. But, *men.* All immigrants I would guess.'

'What are they testing them for?'

'That is the million dollar question, babe. Here, I got these.'

Charlie sat down with the papers he took from the operations room in the facility.

'Let me have a look at those.' Tara said, and Charlie was only too happy to oblige. He got changed and brushed his teeth in the bathroom before returning.

'Hm, medical tests. But it's difficult to say for what...'

'Yep...'

'It seems like some kind of covert, classified testing, see look at this here...' Tara intimated at the patented crest that was on each sheet. 'When they find out that these are missing...'

'Yep, I'm sure there will be uproar. In fact, they are not the only thing that has gone missing. While I was investigating the labs, Becky disappeared.'

'Really, what, she left you?'

'I don't think so. I went into the building, she was lookout. She was there when I went it, gone when I came out.'
Tara sat up in bed. 'So... what are you doing about it?'
'What can I do? There was a little bit of blood where she was, but there was no trail, it didn't lead anywhere so... it could have been anything. I keep calling but there is no answer.'
'Hm. Come and lie down.' Tara said, but Charlie couldn't relax. He did sit up in bed and checked his phone. Re-checking his WhatsApp's to Becky to see if they had gone through.
Tara reached over and kissed him, putting her hand on his chest.
'Try and sleep, honey.' She said as she turned the light out.
Charlie watched the night sky through the slats in the blinds. He watched the orange neon lights, the telephone wires. The occasional car slowly accelerated along Hythe Road. And here he was again, alone with his thoughts; a dangerous place.

Charlie awoke on Dungeness Beach. The wind was howling and it was dark and grey.
He walked towards the water's edge, but it kept moving further away. There was someone by his side, to his right, but he couldn't move his head to see who it was.
'You couldn't save me, Charlie.'
It was a feminine voice, someone he recognised, someone buried deep in his past.
He kept moving.
'Ere Charlie? Let's get on our toes, yeah?'

He heard the voices, but couldn't find where they were coming from. Charlie changed direction towards the lighthouse. He couldn't control his movements. His movements controlled him. The lighthouse burned bright, powerfully. He was bathed in it's warm glow. He went towards it, at its mercy, praying for its warmth to swallow him up and take him away. He kept walking towards it, closer and closer, he was nearly there, and out of the light came a long spindly arm and a knife thrusting down into his chest, again and again. Ripping through his clothes, ripping the flesh.
'Come on Charlie... it's all just a bit of a laugh...'

Charlie woke, covered in sweat. He heard movement in the hallway that stopped outside of his bedroom. He stayed still and listened.
Quiet footsteps.
He rolled out of bed and crawled silently on all fours to the closed door of the bedroom. He listened to whoever was on the other side.
In a flash, he thrust the door open to see Maddie, scared, staring down at him. He pulled her to him and they both relaxed.
'What are you doing?' Charlie asked.
'Bad dream, dad.'
'Hm. Me too. Come in here.'
Charlie got to his feet and carried his daughter to the king-size bed. dropping her down quietly, so as not to wake Tara or the baby.
'It's going to be OK, dad.' Maddie whispered as they curled up in a cuddle.
Charlie was a little taken aback by what she had said, *wasn't he supposed to be reassuring her?*

'Yes, darling. It will be OK.'

The three of them woke, just after seven, to the sound of baby Ridley wailing in the corner of the room.
Charlie got up to grab her and noticed for the first time Maddie's sheer length stretched out upon the bed. She must have been at least five foot six inches now and her feet had grown to a size seven.
She stirred, as did Tara, who began to prepare the milk for the bubba.
Charlie passed the baby to his wife, before settling back into the bed and turning BabyTV on. Maddie always seemed transfixed by it.
'You know this is for babies, right?' Charlie said.
'Yeah, but I like it. All of the colours and numbers and stuff.'
She glanced at Tara who winked at her, without Charlie noticing. The TV sadly couldn't keep Charlie's attention for very long, so he reached over to check his phone.
Three missed calls and two whatsapps, all from Becky.
It's OK. I'm safe. One of the under -19's pulled me from the building and roughed me up a little. Took me to a trap house somewhere in town. Tied me up, tried to scare me. Then an hour ago, they just let me go. Going home to sleep. We have work to do tomorrow.
A large wave of euphoria washed over Charlie.
Perhaps Maddie was right. Perhaps he was going to be OK. Perhaps everything would be OK.

The family had a lazy morning where the three girls stayed in bed and Charlie went downstairs to cook them breakfast. They laughed and joked before

Charlie took Maddie back to Ashford station, so she could return to her mum's.

As always, he felt that twinge of sadness when she left, but these days, it was tempered with the fact that she was going to come back.

She was going to come back.

He put it down to the fact that since he had stopped throwing drink down his neck, as soon as she disappeared, he was able to rationalise his thoughts and fears more. Of course, when you are drinking heavily, it is impossible to do that. She would leave, Charlie would drink and he would be imagining the worst. Paranoia would set in, fear would become king and panic, his best friend.

Now, he stayed calm.

Yes, he felt he could really use a drink right now, but he knew in his heart of hearts that maybe the first drink would be good, calm his nerves, but the second and third and fourth, would just send him into a downward spiral. Then tomorrow morning, the fear would start up all over again.

He knew there was a meeting in Willesborough, at 10.30am, so he grabbed a coffee and headed to it. Better to be safe than sorry.

'My first husband was a womaniser and an alcoholic, but he also used amphetamines, speed. When he wasn't in the pub, he was with other women. Then he would come home, take more drugs, drink more, and then start on me. He wanted me to leave and would get violent. He used an iron on me once…' The woman stopped for a moment to pull up her hoodie over half of her face. 'One time he smashed a bottle in anger and then tried to…'

Charlie stopped his eyes from widening at the desperation of this story. No matter how low he felt or how bad his life got, there was always someone who had it worse.
The woman went on to talk about how she drank during her pregnancy, due to fear of her husband, and gave her kid some form of lifelong issue because of it. Charlie had zoned out by this point. It was like he needed AA to help recharge the batteries, to recalibrate the system, once it had occurred, his thoughts switched to matters at hand.
The facility he and Becky had entered was undertaking some form of illegal tests. It had to be something dodgy, something that they shouldn't be doing, otherwise why hide it an industrial estate in Folkestone?
Like the Border Facility in Ashford, they were hiding in plain sight, hoping that the residents wouldn't bat an eyelid as they went about whatever covert activities they wanted.
Charlie waited for the meeting to finish, then got in his car and dialled Jacko's number.
'Hey Jacko, how's it going?'
'Ah, good buddy. Busy! How are you?'
'Yeah not bad. Just wanted to ask you, what do you know about a medical facility just off Dover Road?'
There was silence on the other end of the line, then a muffled noise.
'Jacko? You know about this?'
'Ah, no sorry… just making sure I don't burn my lunch. I don't think there is a medical facility, just some old factories. I think sometimes the dealers take up residence there when they need somewhere to hide out.'

‘Yeah, maybe, but there’s definitely more going on than that. Come on, you must know something?’ Charlie pushed him, not wanting to reveal his full hand. He was sure Jacko was stalling on him.
‘I’ll see what I can dig up. But let me give you a piece of advice, Charlie…’
‘Yeah?’
‘I’m serious. You want to be careful sniffing out there. You know? Worst case, your dealing with Albanian and Afghan and God knows what else drug dealers. Best case scenario, they will carve a hole in your chest where your heart used to be…’
‘Nice…’
‘Whatever it is, if you are sniffing around, the repercussions as you well know, could be much worse.’
‘Thanks for that, Jacks.’
‘I’m only warning you, Charlie, because I care about you.’
‘What happened to fighting the good fight? Trying to help people and get to the bottom of illicit activities? Aren’t cases like this the reason we get into the force in the first place?’
‘Some things… as I have said to you before, you cannot touch. Sure the little drug dealers around town… do what you got to do. Fight crime to your hearts content. But some things are better left alone.’
‘On that note, I’ve heard that it’s the McCarthy brothers running some illegal operation with the refugees off the beach. But it’s too big for these two, no matter how hard they think they are. From what I understand, it's professionally run, with medical experts, ambulances and so on. You sure you don’t know anything?’

There was a pause.
'Why are you so interested anyway?'
'So, this guy, Johnny McCarthy pulled up to my house, assaulted Tara in my home.'
'Are you fucking kidding me? Why didn't you report it?'
'What's the point? So he gets a warning or something? A caution? Maybe a suspended sentence? I met the guy too. There was this young guy, Ahmed, being sick, like violently sick, in real pain along the Harbour. This McCarthy character pulled up and told us to move along. I didn't. It's safe to say I am not his favourite person.'
'Hm. I would avoid the facility, Charlie. And keep a low profile. You may not think it, but these guys are pretty unpleasant. He is a spiteful character, a clever bastard too. We have had him a couple of times and each time he has wriggled out of it.'
'OK, well if you hear anything that may help me, let me know. OK, boss?'
'Sure thing, Charlie. But you have heard my advice, right?'
'Right.'
Charlie put the phone down and went back home. He had agreed to take Tara and the baby out for lunch, as they hadn't really spent any time together since the birth.
When he entered the house, he felt relaxed and could hear shuffling upstairs which suggested that Tara was getting ready.
'Oh look at this, Mr Charlie Stone, back early for a date!' Tara said sarcastically.
'It's the new me, sweetheart.' Charlie said, leaning over to kiss her.

She was looking great, her long blonde hair down in curls. She was also wearing a little black dress and given that she had just given birth, she looked awesome.
'Can you just put this necklace on for me?' Tara asked.
Charlie obliged, breathing in her scent and taking the opportunity to kiss her on the neck.
'Now, now, not sure I'll be ready for that yet.'
Charlie smirked.
'What?'
'Well, there's more than one way to skin a cat,' he said.
'Leave the pussy out of it,' she whispered, 'Let's just have a nice lunch, eh?'
'Woah, you said pussy!'
'Come on Mister! Grab Ridley please, too. She is already in the car seat.'

Steve McCarthy made his excuses to his brother and Ron, before walking into Folkestone.
He much preferred going out for a few casual drinks on his own. It gave him time to collect his thoughts and to recharge.
He loved his brother. He couldn't deny that Johnny's exuberance and cutting, searing entrepreneurial vision had brought him a good life. It had. The problem was, it had all come at a cost.
Steve was too tired to play the old game in his head of whether being a McCarthy brother was worth it. There were perks, there were pitfalls. Either way, it made no difference they were what they were and there was no going back. That ship had sailed. He had a choice for a different life, he could have stayed…

he chose to go out. To follow his brother, to try and save him.
He had failed. On the other hand, nobody in this town, ever messed with him.
He walked into Skuba bar that overlooked the English Channel. It had been given a recent makeover and the gaudy red sofas had been replaced by pseudo-acquatic blue ones. The vibe however was the same. The disco lights, the sticky floor, the European dance music. He felt like he was in a little bubble here. Far away from the troubles of his real life.
'Estrella please,' Steve said to the barman.
He looked around and as it was lunchtime on a Friday, the place was relatively empty. There was a couple outside in the smoking area, while the bar area and dancefloor was empty, bar one middle-aged lady dancing.
The barman passed Steve his drink and he gulped it a bit too eagerly, polishing off over half the pint in one go.
He surprised himself and the barman too, who gave him a cheeky smile.
'That went down quickly! Fancy another?'
'Yeah. Best do,' Steve returned, while the barman smiled and plucked another pint glass from under the counter.
'Something bothering you?' the barman said smiling again at him.
'Oh, yeah. I mean, not really… just you know family drama.'
'Oh god. Tell me about it!' the barman said in an overly camp voice. 'They are the friends you don't get to choose, right?'
'Yep, something like that.'

‘Here’s your pint and have a cheeky shot on me.’ The barman got out two fluorescent glasses and lined them up on the bar.
‘Oh, no… it’s OK…’ Steve tried, but the barman was not to be deterred.
‘Come on, you look like you need a day off!’
The two of them downed their shot and Steve McCarthy felt the corner of his lips turn upwards for the first time in a while.

Charlie and Tara drove into Ashford and went to one of the new restaurants in Elwick Place. Charlie marvelled at the modernity of this new complex, it was a distinct improvement.
'Italian?' Tara suggested.
'Sure thing.'
Charlie had done this many times before, but of course this time it felt somewhat different. Whereas his sole focus historically had been on ensuring Tara had a great time, this had now shifted to making sure Ridley was safe. If they had a good time, that was nice, but realistically all decisions were no longer about them anymore.
‘Shall we sit over there? There’s space for the pushchair…’ Tara bargained with the young male waiter and Charlie smiled and followed along.
They settled into their seats, which again took longer than it used to, not that either of them minded.
‘How are you feeling, T?’ Charlie asked.
‘Not bad at all, definitely on the mend,’ Her face however told a different story that Charlie was obviously incapable of understanding. The pain and sacrifice that any woman has to go through is something unfathomable when you really analysed it.

I mean, the whole body shifts and changes. The bones in your abdomen, your hips have to move to make way for the baby. Not to mention the physicality of birth. That's before you even got into the emotional toll it must have taken. It really is a good thing they don't tell you the full story of labour before the event. That said, it would almost certainly bring down the number of teen pregnancy if these mothers were privy to the horrors that Charlie had witnessed during the birth of his two daughters.

'Oh, that's good,' Charlie returned, thinking it best to keep his thoughts to himself.

'This case then…'

'Well, let's not talk about it here?' Is that OK?'

'Can I get you any drinks, sir?' The waiter said from behind him.

'See what I mean? You never know who is listening in…' Charlie smiled at Tara, who nodded in agreement.

'I'll have a San Pellegrino, orange,' Tara stated.

'Sparkling water, please.'

The waiter nodded and scurried off towards the back of the building.

'OK, I'll change subject. Have you ever heard of synaesthesia, Char?'

'Refresh my memory?'

'People who can see emotions and feelings in colours, shapes and numbers… that sort of thing.'

'What? Like Rain Man?' As soon as Charlie said it, he was glad Becky wasn't here, as she would have made some smartarse comment about him never leaving the eighties. She was probably right, mind.

'No, not like *rain man*, Charlie. That is autism. High – level. It's more a confusion of the senses… where

the neural pathways get a bit confused, but can cause some amazing results, a bit like autism in a way…'
'Give me an example.'
'Well, the reason I bring it up is Maddie. She and I spoke last night while you were out and she said to me that she sometimes feels colours…'
'Right…'
'Like, she said she can see how you're feeling and could sense my anxiety about you know... the…'
'Yes, I'm dealing with that, don't worry…'
'I know, I know… that's not why I brought it up. It's just I felt obviously, a bit out of sorts, and she said that I was feeling green….like a dark green, and so she wanted to brush my hair.'
'That's so sweet of her… so, she sees *feelings* in *colours?*'
'Sort of, but she can also predict things. If you are somewhere far away in a different town, she reckons she knows how you are feeling. She talked about your… mood changes and how you go from one extreme to another…'
'What me?' Charlie smiled, as the waiter placed the drinks down on the table. 'So why are you telling me this?'
'Because it's amazing, Charlie. She has a gift! I just want to make sure it isn't like… beaten out of her, or she is made to feel bad about it. She can't help it. If it's harnessed in the right way, it might give her a real advantage in the world.'
'Sounds to me like you're saying my daughter is a witch!'
They both smiled, Tara sensing that her partner was joking.
They ordered food and continued to talk. Ridley

didn't cry once and slept for most of the meal, which pleased them both, as they needed the time together.
As they left, Charlie noticed the Picturehouse cinema next door.
'Fancy catching a movie?' he asked.
'Erm… what about the baby?'
'Ah yeah, good point. Can't she come too? She won't know what's going on in a Marvel movie…'
'I don't think so. Let's go home and snuggle in bed…'
'You don't have to ask me twice!' Charlie said, pulling Tara towards him.
'Not like that, mister!'
The three went back home and went upstairs. Ridley nestled comfortably between the two of them, while Tara found something for them to watch on Netflix. It wasn't long before Ridley fell asleep and Tara gently moved her to her moses basket.
Charlie and Tara snuggled together, Charlie respectfully not trying to up it a gear, but just enjoying the new found closeness. With the stability of an alcohol-free life and his family around him, for the first time in many years, he felt secure.
Happy even.
He closed his eyes and fell into a deep sleep as Tara gently rubbed the scars on his upper arms and torso.

The room was swirling in pinks, pastel blues and oranges.
The bass from the sound system was pounding through Steve McCarthy's body as he twirled and pirouetted on the makeshift dancefloor.
Steve couldn't stop grinning. He was drunk and for the first time in a long time, felt like a weight had

been lifted.
'So are you from Folkestone then?' the barman asked, leaning into Steve's ear.
'Yeah. All my life.'
'Me too. Surprised I haven't met you before.' The barman said, clutching a small glass of vodka and coke to his chest before taking a sip through a black straw.
'Well, why would you?'
'There's a pretty big gay scene here, but we all tend to know each other…'
The barman stared at Steve to gauge his reaction.
'Oh, no. Erm, I'm not… you know…' Steve fumbled.
'Of course you're not mate. Just forget it and have a dance!'
The barman who had now finished his shift and spun around in front of Steve. His ripped, blue t-shirt hung lazily from his body and his skinny jeans hugged his body nicely.
Steve swallowed back the feelings that were rising.
He couldn't. Not here, not in public.
Steve started feeling a little nauseous and went outside to get some fresh air. He walked around the corner of the building and felt the urge to throw up. He wretched once and then again but nothing came up.
'You OK, hun?' It was the barman again.
Steve looked up and down the road, it was early evening and luckily, the road was deserted.
'Yeah, I'm OK. Don't know what came over me…'
'Well, what are the odds? A taxi over the road. Are you coming?' the barman said as he skipped towards the waiting vehicle.
Steve smiled and followed the barman into the car.

They sat down in the backseat and the barman moved towards him.
'Not here, not now.' Steve said quietly.
The barman tutted and told the driver his address. As soon as they arrived, Steve paid with a twenty-pound note and the two men made their way to the barman's flat, located just off Canterbury Road.
As soon as they were inside the door, Steve grabbed the boy and began kissing him as hard as he could. The boy gave as good as he got, tearing at Steve's shirt and his belt buckle, whilst leading him into the bedroom.
A few moments later, both men were naked and pricked with sweat. The young barman was kissing Steve's body and eventually took his length in his mouth.
Steve gasped and shuddered as the warm sensations fluttered through his body, pulling him towards the edge of climax.
Anxious not to ruin the moment, Steve pulled the boy from him and the lay on his front in front of him. The boy needed no encouragement, kissing Steve's back, before gently entering him. Steve lay in a mixture of elation and shame, his head on his arms, willing the boy to drive himself harder and faster into him.

16

When Charlie awoke, it was dark outside and he felt that immediate sense of panic…when you fall asleep during the day. *Where was he? What time was it?*

Tara and Ridley were not there, but he could hear the sound of the TV downstairs.

He took a moment to settle himself and then to check his phone. He had three calls from an unknown number.

He placed the phone back down and got his clothes on before going downstairs.

The phone rang again as he was halfway down the stairs. He turned around and went back up. An unknown call once more.

'Hello?'

'Charlie! You have been looking for me!' a cockney cockiness to the voice. Johnny McCarthy.

'Who is this please?'

'Don't play silly, Charlie. You know full well who it is. The fella who still smells of your wife…'

'You have been hiding away, Johnny.'

'Not so, Charlie. Not so at all. That's why I wanted to talk to you. You have been snooping about, I hear. So that slag you work with tells us…'

'Is that so?'

'Listen, I will make this easy for you. Can you meet me in half an hour, the old Dover Railway Club?'

'*Dover?*'

'Yeah, why not eh? Nice to slum it sometimes. See you there.'

Charlie was awash with anger and rage. He wanted to meet him, he needed to find this guy and warn him off. Get him away from his family.

'Charlie, you OK up there?'
'Yes, babe just grabbing my wallet, then I'm popping out for an hour or so. Maybe two.'
'Oh, that's a shame. Was going to get dinner on…'
'Go ahead babe, like I said, I won't be long. Just got a lead in this case. I might have found the man from the other day.'
Tara shuddered at the thought.
'I'm sorry, Tara. I should have thought…'
'No, he's a creep. Good, go and sort him out, will you?' she smiled and kissed him on the lips as he headed for the door.
'Don't be long, Charlie. I love you.' Tara said, glowing with joy.
'I love you too.'

'Are you OK?' the barman said.
'I'm fine.'
'You don't seem fine… first time?'
'No.'
'Are you married?'
'Just leave it will you?' Steve hadn't moved lying on his back, his body naked and cold in the late afternoon.
The barman moved towards Steve slowly. He stroked his head and tried to hold him. Steve began to weep and moved into the boy's lap. Crying harder and harder.
'It's OK. It's OK! I wasn't that bad was I?' the barman mused.
Steve looked up and they both laughed.
'Whatever it is, it's better if you can talk about it…'
'Ah… it's nothing. Just… my brother. He's uh… a bit old school. You know? Doesn't really appreciate

a… different way of life, if you catch my drift?'
'Well, what do you care what your brother thinks? Its 2022, baby!' the barman said with mock cheerfulness.
'Yeah, it's not that simple…'
'Why?'
'He is… a powerful man…'
'Ooh, like a businessman?'
Steve smiled and went to put his boxer shorts back on.
'Yeah, something like that.'
'Oh, like a gangster?'
'I think I better go.' Steve said, hurrying to put his clothes on.
'Listen, we had fun right? Right? Do you not want to see me again?'
Steve looked down at his belt buckle as he rushed to put his shirt and jacket on. He flattened his hair to one side in the mirror and made himself slightly presentable for the outside world.
Steve turned and looked at the boy.
'It was great, but if you see me in the street, ever, don't talk to me. I mean that.'
'Oh, whatever. You're in denial, babe.'
'Listen… I'm…'
'Just fuck off… shut the door on your way out, you bloody weirdo.'
The boy was picking up a tobacco pouch and finding his rizla papers.
Steve bowed his head and left the flat, wiping the final tears from his eyes.

En route to Dover, Charlie rang Becky.
'How are you doing, kiddo?'
'Yeah, OK. Bit shaken up by the other day, but

uhm…yeah feeling better.'
'Beck, I'm sorry for…'
'Listen, save it, old timer. We had an agreement to meet and it didn't work out. It's not on you. Like I said, it was nothing too bad, a bit of a kicking, that's all.'
'Well, thanks for being…uh… understanding. Anyway, guess who just called me? Johnny McCarthy. Wants to meet.'
'Oh jeez, that will be dangerous, Charlie. I'm coming with.'
'Yes, sounds like a plan. He wants to meet in Dover. Railway Club?'
'Well at least it's in public. Did he say what he wanted?'
'Nope. Talked about us being at the factory…'
'How did he know you were there?'
'Well, he reckons that… that… you may have said something…'
'Bullshit, Charlie. I didn't say a word. They didn't even interrogate me, or ask me anything!'
'OK, sure. I believe you. Listen, how about you meet me just up the road from the club and we can talk then?'
'I'll text you when I'm there.'

Charlie put the phone down and continued along the old motorway towards Dover.
Past Folkestone, the stretch of M20 into East Kent becomes the A20, and the scenery transitions into something rather picturesque. Once past Samphire Hoe, the hills open out into the valley and the glistening sea provides the backdrop. Dover Harbour stretches out in the distance and the old part town

looks somewhat magical.
Charlie drove along the seafront, past the Booking Hall and the regenerated Harbour area, with its trendy bars, before taking a left towards the older parts of town.
He arrived and parked the car one hundred metres or so up the road from the Railway Club. He looked inside and saw a thrum of activity. Lots of men talking, drinking but from the outside he couldn't see the face of Johnny McCarthy.
He walked up the road and awaited Becky's arrival. She said she was a few minutes away and to wait at the top of the road, so he did. She pulled up and Charlie went across to the passenger side and got in.
'Hey,' she said.
'Hey. Jeez!' Charlie noticed the marks and cuts across her face. 'I thought you said they didn't rough you up that bad!'
'They didn't, it's OK, Charlie.'
Charlie silently seethed.
'Who was it?'
'The under 19's. What we didn't realise was that although a few of them were hanging around on their bikes, they were also dotted around the facility as lookouts. I think they saw us as soon as we came in.'
'Right. And then picked you off...'
'Anyway, I think you need to go in alone to meet McCarthy. I will be outside if you need me.'
'Yes. I don't think he will be happy if we both rock up. OK. Wish me luck.'
'Keep your cool, Charlie. No matter what he says. He will have his goons with him. See what he has to say, try and glean any intel, then get out of there.'
'Right you are, boss!'

'Sorry, but… you know what I mean!'
Charlie opened the door and headed into the dark night, into the unknown.

Tara sat with the baby on her knee, cooing and kissing the little pink bundle. Being apart from Charlie was not something she enjoyed, but it did give her time to reflect on what had happened with her and the baby. To be honest, she was still a little in a bit of a 'dream state,' as if the world wasn't really real. How did she get to be a mother, in charge of the most precious cargo in the world?
She pulled the baby into her, hard. She wasn't going to ever let the bubba down.
Tara thought she heard something at the front door, so she placed the baby back in the basket. There it was again, this time louder. It was the metal letterbox clanging together. She went to the door to find no one there but the porch door and the gate at the end of their front garden was wide open.
Charlie went out the back, though. Didn't he? He wouldn't have left the gate like that though, would he?
Tara put the kettle on in the kitchen and as she waited, she once again saw movement through the stained-glass in the front door.
She was shaken and scared, but she wasn't to be bullied. She grabbed a kitchen knife from the drawer and went back to the front door.
She pulled it open to see a young man, dressed in black, with a hood covering most of his face.
'What do you want?'
'Err… missus…' the juvenile spoke in a faux gangster-chav accent.

'What is it?' Tara shouted.
In the few moments it had taken to open the door and interact with the boy, two of his gang members had slid their wiry frames through Tara and Charlie's ventilation window that was open upstairs. Their feet were now thundering down Tara's staircase. She yelped in fright and fell to her knees, dropping the knife in the process.
The last boy at the front door kicked her back inside the property and closed the door quietly behind him.
They surrounded her, pulling her into the kitchen, two of them holding her arms and legs, while the other boy grabbed the top of her black leggings, pulling them down. In the melee, he noticed the large, industrial-sized sanitary pad, the blood, and stopped.
'Fucking sket,' the boy spat on her, but left her leggings on.
Tara couldn't fight. She was too afraid, too weak, too scared. Like rats upon a rare and precious morsel of food, the boys set upon her with their tiny blades.
'Don't touch my baby! Leave my baby alone!' she screeched as the boys did their work.
Death by a thousand cuts, as Ridley lay sleeping in the room next door.

Steve took a deep breath and pulled the infant from the backseat of his car.
Normally the little blighters were crying their heads off by now, but this one was as silent as a mouse.
He looked at her face, eyes closed. The peace, the tranquility.
Steve envied the little girl.
He carried her through the woodland, around the orchard and to the small shed at the back of the large

property.
As he approached, he noticed the homely orange glow coming from the shed, there was a shuffle of movement, then the makeshift door flung open, to reveal the man in the long white cloak.
It was surreal. Every time Steve did the drop off, he had to pinch himself that this was actually real, actually happening. He felt that he had fallen into the Hobbit or some other fantasy for a brief moment.
The baby in his arms woke at the sound of the door.
'Sshh… it's OK, it's OK…' Steve said, consoling the little one in his arms.
'Steve, thank you. Thank you. Pass him here,' the man said.
'Her. A girl…'
'Ah, a beautiful, wonderful baby girl. Come here.'
The man took the bundle and moved towards the shed.
'Are you coming in, Steve?'
'Nah, not today.'
'I see. I am afraid we're getting to capacity now, so I think we have to stop the… arrangement… for a while.'
'Oh really, are you sure?' Steve was visibly perturbed, anxious.
'I'm afraid so. For now. Hopefully not for long though. How is your brother? Is he still asking about me?'
'You know I can't talk about that side of the business…'
'…I didn't ask you about your business.' The old man said softly.
'You know… well, he's still wild and uncontrollable. Won't listen. Takes risks. Every threat eliminated.

You know? Which is why…'
'He has always been the same. Tortured. Inside, deep inside, I think there is a good soul, it's just buried… but he must never know about this… here. OK?'
'God, no! No, it would make him worse.'
'It would.'
There was a brief awkward pause between the two men.
'Well, I had best be off.'
'Johnny, stay calm, try and stay happy. I will be in touch soon.'
Johnny nodded and walked away from the old shed towards the wooded area. He felt deflated and angry. He couldn't believe that this little setup was over for now. It made him feel good, a sense of redemption for all of the evil that him and his brother had been caught up in.
He shoved his hands in his pocket and checked his phone.
No missed calls. No texts.

Charlie entered the Railway Club and scanned the room for Johnny McCarthy.
He felt his blue intense eyes boring into him from a booth towards the back. He was sitting with two goons, with one space for Charlie to sit down.
'Hello, Charlie. Pull up a pew.' Johnny said cheerfully.
'What do you want?'
'Now, now, Charlie. You haven't even learned about your big surprise yet and you're getting shirty…'
Charlie was raging under the surface, simmering with heat. He wanted to tear the guy in front of him limb from limb for violating his wife, for spreading this

darkness through East Kent.
'I don't like surprises.'
'No, and I don't think you will like this one either, Charlie. However, I did warn you and I did make it very clear that you shouldn't be snooping about in my affairs. Did I not?'
Charlie said nothing, but held Johnny's gaze.
'I did. Now you fucking ignored that warning, and came steaming in again, didn't you? And I very kindly spared that little rat girl assistant of yours because... well, just because... but I couldn't let lightning strike twice Charlie. I hope you understand that.'
Charlie was beginning to panic.
'If you have hurt my kids or my wife...I...'
'Shut up, son. You are fucking boring.'
Johnny checked his texts and nodded.
'I want to show you something, Charlie. But just remember when I do, my friend Ron here, has got a gun pointed at your bollocks.'
Charlie felt the gun thrust into his groin and it briefly took the air from his gut.
'After I show you this. I'm going to leave. Then I don't want to ever see your fat fucking face again, Charlie. I hope you listen this time.'
Johnny turned the phone around and showed Charlie a brief image.
A flash.
Blood.
Blonde hair.
Murder.
The world moved in slow motion as Charlie heaved himself up, pulling the table with him. Johnny McCarthy moved swiftly to the back door as

Charlie's arms flailed wildly and Ron smothered him with his large, bear-like frame.

17

Had he known all the things he knew now, he wondered whether he would have agreed to come this far.
Walking into the sea seemed like a viable option on more than one occasion in his life. His dad, when he was sick, wanted to walk into the desert and never return. Charlie's companion was the sea. He loved it. He wanted to walk into it and never return.
It made him realise that every stupid decision he had made, every risk, every failure, was small in comparison to something as wild and untameable as the ocean. For a moment, a very brief moment, it made him feel OK. Like he was insignificant and the bad decisions were momentary and that there were bigger things in the world.
Everything he had done, in his own head, had come from a place of good. To try and make the world a better place, to improve it, to set the record straight. But every outcome had brought death, sadness, destruction.
At best, pain.
He didn't deserve to be in the world.
He was better out of it.

'Dad? It's time.'
Charlie came to, in the front room of his house. His mother was there, Becky and Maddie, both dressed in black. Charlie nodded and followed what was left of his family, out of the room.
The setting was beautiful. White flowers adorned the small chapel, low sunlight dappled the doorway, a cool breeze swept through the mourners. Charlie was

in the dream state as he spoke to the guests, Tara's family and friends, as they spoke to him. But the lights were on and nobody was home. Like a night without sleep, he was looking at his grim reality through what felt like a thick pane of glass.

'... To lose her life in such tragic circumstances, a bungled burglary, when Tara Stone had so much to offer the world still...'

Charlie knew what he had to do...

'... leaving behind a doting husband and two daughters, Maddie and Ridley...'

He was going to execute the final plan...

'A sweet, loving and caring young woman, who only did her best for her family and will be sorely missed by all who knew her...'

There will be two more parts to the Charlie Stone story. Revenge and then a final goodbye. That's how it will end.

'... I would now like to invite Charlie Stone, Tara's husband, to say a few words...'

For the first time in three days, Charlie felt something other than numbness. He got up from the pew and made his way to the front of the chapel. He took a piece of paper from his jacket pocket and opened it up.
'Tara Stone was a wonderful woman... she.... She

had many incredible traits that…'
Charlie stopped himself and took a deep breath. He folded the paper up again and placed it back into his pocket.
'My life has been a series of tragic events, laced together with moments of beauty and grace and wonderment.
Tara epitomised those moments. She was an angel, full of grace, full of kindness. In moments like these, people often wax lyrical about men and women who weren't actually that great…'
A member of Tara's extended family coughed and shifted uncomfortably in their seat.
'… I mean it's true. But, in Tara's case she was all of those things. And how do you judge a life? I guess you judge it on the impact it has on other people. And the minute I met her; I had a feeling that there was something special about her. Like a shell with a pearl inside it, that just needed to be opened. Marriage and parenthood brought that out of her. She immediately accepted my daughter, Maddie, and became a brilliant stepmum, always there to help her, always there to support her.
The world is a better place for Tara Stone being in it. I am just sorry for not being there to protect her, for bringing her danger… for…'
Charlie stopped and nodded at the vicar. He had nothing more to say. As he sat down his mother leant across to him with words of encouragement.
The service ended and at Charlie's request the song 'See Her Out' by Francis and the Lights played. The bass of the keyboard hook was loud and hit Charlie firmly in the chest. The lights dimmed and the small claret-coloured curtains slowly drew across the pine

coffin.
To Charlie's left, as he squeezed tears from his eyes, he noticed movement.
A white soul wrapped in a black dress was dancing in the sterile room. Legs were gliding gracefully, arms were moving magnificently.
It was Maddie.
Tara's family looked across bemused, but Maddie was in an ethereal world, connected to a higher energy. She was grace… purity personified, eyes closed in time with the tune. Tara's tune.
She slid nearer the centre of the room and spun to the beat. Her eyes were still closed; she was enveloped entirely by the sound, her movements involuntary, entirely part of her gift.
Charlie smiled.
As the tune broke down in the middle-eight, Maddie opened her eyes and indicated for her father to dance with her.
He did.
He got up from the pew and took up his daughter's hand, supporting her, spinning her. He tried to move with her but he was like a drunken bear trying to stay in time .
For the final part of the song, a number of the guests had risen from their seats and were dancing to the music too. Seeing Tara out, with joy and with beauty, rather than sadness.
All too quickly, the moment was over, the lights were up and they were back in the cold harsh light of the chapel being ushered out like a procession, while a group of other mourners waited impatiently for their fifteen minutes outside.
Charlie, Maddie and his mother, walked slowly

outside to the remembrance garden.
'Your dancing was beautiful, Mad,' Charlie whispered in her ear. For the first time in a long while, he raised a smile.
'Thanks, dad. Honestly, though, I can't help it. It wasn't really appropriate, was it?'
'Who cares what these people think, eh? They didn't know T like we did, and she would have *loved* it.' Charlie squeezed her hand as Maddie smiled at him.
Tara's father was standing at the other side of the garden and continued to look over. Eventually he made his move with Tara's mother and spoke.
'Charlie,'
'Hi, Alan.'
'I always said you were a rotten egg…'
'Don't say that about my dad!' Maddie piped up. Alan was not to be told though.
'Had she never met you, none of this would have happened. She would be safe with us, and she would still be here! It's you with your bloody… *you…*'
He stopped and Charlie nodded. He wasn't in the mood, the comfortable numbness had returned, the familiar feeling that it was all his fault.
'If it wasn't for Charlie, you wouldn't have Ridley. And had Tara have been happy with you at home, she would have stayed there, *Alan*. Anyway, this is neither the time nor the place and as her father you should know better. Come on Charlie, Maddie, let's go.' Charlie's mother said emphatically. With force, she removed the brake from Ridley's pushchair and headed out towards the car park.
Charlie couldn't help but raise an eyebrow. It wasn't often his mother went into bat for him, but she had. Charlie was impressed as the four of them walked

swiftly back to the car.

18

The phone was buzzing again.

It was the new soundtrack to Charlie's life, buzz, buzz, buzz, buzz.

He watched the colours light up on the phone, before fading to its usual resting darkness. He wondered if anyone had ever slept so much, that they ended up dying from over-sleeping? Was that a thing? Maybe it was. It was weird too, how the more he stayed in bed, the more lethargic he became.

Surely after weeks in bed, you would have enough energy to get up and get out of it?

He pressed the button on the PlayStation controller and watched the console burst into life. The familiar blue light flashed on and he shuffled himself up to a vague seated position. Well, it was more a lying position with his head cranked up by pillows so that he could see the screen.

He was currently playing a game called, 'Ghosts of Tsushima.' A samurai reclaiming his decimated island from Mongol invasion and subsequent rule. It made him happy. He longed for a life this simple. Just going from village to village, slaying the invaders.

If he died, so be it. He died with honour protecting something that he loved.

Charlie heard footsteps coming up the stairs. He sighed and hid the controller underneath the duvet and turned the TV off.

'Right, Charlie. Ridley is changed and fed. She is napping downstairs. I have made you a carrot soup and it's currently in the slow cooker. If you leave it for an hour or so it will be ready for dinner time. I need to get back and take the dog for a walk.'

'OK, thanks mum.'
'Have you got that PlayStation on again?' his mum looked up at the light on the machine and sighed. 'For goodness sake, Charlie! It is like your fifteen again! At some point, like *now*, you need to get up and get on with life. You know that don't you? I'm seventy-five Charlie, I can't keep coming around and doing this for you.'
Charlie looked at his mother through glassy-eyes. 'Sure, mum.'
'I know it's been tough for you, but you need to get back in the swing of things. It's been a month since...'
'Since my wife was murdered?'
'Charlie, come on...'
'OK, cool. I'll get back to it tomorrow. Whatever *it* is. I forgot there was a time-limit on these things. One month, then sort your shit out and get back in the game!'
'That's not what I meant...'
'No, you're right. What's wrong with me? I do need to get a grip.'
'Charlie, I just.... I just want you to be happy, OK?'
'Hm. That ship has sailed.'
'You have two daughters, they both need their father.'
'Maddie's got a new step-dad. He'll be a better role model than me, I'm sure.'
'You are her *father*, Charlie.'
'Thanks, mum!'
'Right, there's no point in arguing with you when you are in this mood. I'm off. I will pop in tomorrow. Do you want me to bring Ridley up here, so you can... play?'

'No, it's fine. Thanks again.'
'OK. See you tomorrow.'
Charlie's mother left and he turned the TV back on. He clicked on the game icon and let it load, before heading downstairs to bring his daughter up to lie in bed with him for the rest of the day.
The phone rang again. It was Becky. Charlie picked up the phone and turned his notifications to silent, before placing it back on the side.
Time to slay some Mongol warriors!

Becky put the phone down again and took a deep breath.
Bloody Charlie Stone!
He had suffered, lord knows he had, but why did that mean he couldn't pick up the sodding phone?
Becky walked through Folkestone town centre, as she had become accustomed to do most days. Under the guise of a Christmas shopper, she was using this down time, thanks to Charlie's disappearance from the face of the earth, to do some much needed reconnaissance.
What she had noticed was interesting. The under-19's were still out in full force.
There were potentially five or six places where groups of three or four girls and boys would congregate in the town centre.
This was normal.
They were still distributing different forms of narcotics to many different people, however, there was one striking and notable difference to the activity in the past few months, and that was that there was at least one Afghan male that stayed with them or, came to meet them throughout the day.

It didn't appear from Becky's limited information that they were passing anything between them, if they were it was just verbal information, nothing else.
Becky picked up the phone again to call Charlie. She was desperate to relay her theory about the Afghans and the under-19's to him, but it was to no avail, he still wasn't answering.
What would Charlie do in this situation?
He would go rogue and do what he thought was best.
And that is what she would do too.

The McCarthy boys sat in the gloom of the Railway Club. It was one thirty in the afternoon on a Thursday, so the club had only a handful of punters in.
'You would think given how the operation is going, Johnny, that we could meet up somewhere other than this dump,' Steve said to his brother, who took a long slug from his pint of beer.
'Nothing like a nice cold beer, eh, Steve? Get yourself one, why don't you?'
'No, you know what I'm like. If I have one I can't stop…'
'Then don't stop… we can have a right old session, like old times!'
'No, that's… that's not a good idea, Johnny…'
'Why? What's wrong with having a nice beer with your brother?'
'It never ends well.' Steve said quietly.
'Well fuck it, I might stay here all day. I love it here. And in answer to your question, the reason we meet here, is because… one… it is quiet, and no-one knows us in this dump. It's all fucking Albanians and Romanians running ops here and they are fucking

welcome to it. Two… Never forget your roots, Johnny. Working. Class. Roots.'
'Yeah, I won't, but there's got to be somewhere else… what about one of these little villages along the A20…'
'Not worth it, too conspicuous. Anyway, we are here now, and I wanted to discuss a few things with you. Now the 'boat party' as I like to call it, seems to be easing off. In a few weeks, all of the testing will be done and basically, our services won't be required anymore. In effect, our contract will be ended with her majesty.'
Steve's phone rang with a number that he didn't recognize. He answered and got up from the table.
'Hey, hun! It's Ray Ray from Skuba the other day…'
'How the fuck did you get this number?'
'I hope you don't mind, but I took it off your phone when you were asleep…'
'You can't call me…' Steve whispered.
'Who's that, eh?' Johnny asked, a smile curling at the corner of his lips.
'No-one, Johnny. Listen, delete this number. I fucking mean it.' Steve said, his voice rising.
'Listen, fuck your brother! You hear me, fuck him! You know you want to meet me again…'
Stevie took a deep breath. He did want to meet him again. He wanted to meet him now. He wanted to hold him and…
'Call this number again and I'll have you fucking killed. You hear me?' Steve said loudly putting the phone down.
'Fucking crackheads, nothing to worry about Johnny…' Steve said.
'I see. Well, back to business, Stevie. It is a problem

for the finances when the contract ends.'
'Really? Demand for our products has never been higher… we can't sell enough of the stuff…'
'Yeah, but if we want to make *serious* money…'
'Is the money we make not serious enough?'
'Steve, this is the problem with you, no ambition.'
'I have ambition, but if it's money you want, then expand the operation. Let's move over here, down to Ashford. No-one runs things over that way. It's all small-time dealers and hoodlums, very easy…'
'That's not what I want. I want to hear about your operation. Operation Born Again.'
Steve knew it was coming, Johnny couldn't help it.
The fact his brother had something for himself that didn't involve him, no matter what it was, how small, ate him up inside.
'It's off limits, Johnny. I don't know how many times I have to tell you?'
Johnny looked hurt, his eyebrow furrowed. 'But, why?'
'It just is, OK? It makes fuck all anyway…'
'It isn't really about the money…'
'I thought that's what you wanted? More money?'
'Well, yeah and no. I just want to know…'
'I know what you want to know. Johnny, I can't share it. If I share it, then we risk it falling apart. I promise you, I will give you half of whatever we make…'
'I know you will, and I trust you on that, but why can't I be involved?'
'It's not necessarily personal, it's just the guy is shaky, unreliable, *nervy.* He wants total privacy.'
'I can't believe you would betray me like this. My own fucking brother!'
Steve cocked an eyebrow, getting his things together

to leave, 'yeah and don't I bloody know it…'
'What did you say?' Johnny said, getting up from the table.
'Sit down, brother. You may be able to intimidate your girlfriends like that, but not me. I've seen your schtick too often. I'm off. Have another beer, yeah?'
'You are going to regret this, Stevie!'
'I already do.'
Steve walked out of the railway club exasperated and got out his phone.
He went into his phonebook and found the number he wanted.
'Hello, Steve,' the old man's voice said softly.
'Hi, are we still good for tonight?'
'Yes, as discussed.'
'Great. That's great news. I just needed to check.'
'Is everything OK?'
'Yes. Yes. Everything is fine. See you then.'

Ridley was crying downstairs.
The wails came in waves.
She would cry hard and then it would fall away to silence, Charlie's heart would slow and he would relax.
Then moments later, the crying would come louder and faster. Charlie stayed in bed. He felt the need to rise, but his body wouldn't let him.
Ridley's wail turned to a scream, she was in pain.
Charlie lifted the duvet from his withering frame and got to his feet. He hurried downstairs and to the crib, staring at the pink-faced, watery-eyed baby.
He felt shame.
Shame for Tara.
Shame for Ridley.

Shame.

He held the baby to his chest and felt the warmth of her breath. Noticed her tears dissipate, listened to her calm, and felt nothing.

He felt nothing.

The baby was calm, so Charlie placed her back in the crib and went to the kitchen to make Ridley her nightly milk.

19

Becky moved quickly through town.

It was not somewhere she wanted to be and longed for the sanctuary, the safety, of her local boozer. Not to mention the feeling of that first drink, taking the edge off her hangover from yesterday.

She wasn't overdoing it as such, but a lack of focus and motivation had led her back to the arms of that warm, old friend… alcohol.

She nodded at the regulars, the girl behind the bar came around and hugged her, the guys playing pool nodded and grunted at her.

She was at least *somebody* here.

Her icy short was placed in front of her as she checked her look in her pocket mirror and reapplied her lip gloss. She took a large glug of the fluid and immediately felt relief. The edges of her anxiety would soon blur. She would be drinking, comfortable and warm until tomorrow, where she would start the whole cycle again… vowing not to drink when she woke, then feeling the itch around midday and by two or three in the afternoon, knowing that her only destination would be back to the bar.

'All right Bex,' one of the men playing pool nodded at her, smiling. She smiled back, pulling her straw into her mouth with her tongue, maintaining eye contact.

'Hey,' she said coyly, looking out of the window. The man grunted and went back to his pool shot. Becky got out her phone, keeping an eye on the man. He was new to the pub, only the second time she had seen him in here. As she scrolled, she noticed him talking to his friends, looking over in her direction. She felt a flutter fall through her. Like she was alive… a

purpose, a chase, a connection.
She checked the messages she had sent to Charlie. Just like earlier, none of them had been read.
'So, what's your name?' the man asked, he was now standing directly beside her.
'Becky. And you?'
'Rod, pleasure to meet you,' he said, holding out his hand. Becky smirked and took it.
'Very formal, Rod!'
'Well, one must be, when one meets a beautiful lady such as yourself…' The man had a deep voice, almost comical in the pace that the words left his mouth. Like a parody of a lovable Kentish rogue. Becky was intrigued.
'So, Rod, tell me a bit about yourself…'
'Me… oh, nothing much to tell. I work for her majesty's police service, but please don't let that deter…'
'Oh, where do you work?'
'Just in the cells, Folkestone…'
'I see, you may know a friend of mine…'
'Is that so? Does this friend have a name?'
'Charlie. Charlie Stone.'
The room stood still as Rod processed the words. After a moment, his mouth broke into a large grin that spread across his goofy face.
'Charlie! Yeah, I know Charlie…' he said, pulling up a bar stool, next to Becky.
'Have you seen him? I mean recently? I have been trying to get hold of him…'
'Let me tell you a little story about our mutual friend, OK?' Becky nodded and waited with baited breath.
'Once upon a time, Charlie and his best friend Dave Woodward ran the Folkestone nick. They did it

mighty well too, I might add. We won't talk about Dave, he met a very tragic end… but anyways Charlie had this case right, where he was asked to investigate a case of abuse… in a family home…'

'Wait, erm… wasn't Charlie serious crimes? And drugs before that?'

'Very good, Becky. You know your Charlie Stone history. This was a special case, the family were quite… *dangerous* shall we say, and well known in the community. Charlie knew the dad and Dave thought he could get a better response from him than anyone else. So, he sent him.'

'Ah, right…'

'Anyway, beautiful young Becky, prithee may I continue?'

'…Sure?'

'Charlie knew that there had been mounting reports of neglect to do with this one young chap called Arnold. And things had gone very quiet. Dave sent him around to the house where they all lived. He knocked to no avail, but Charlie has this weird sixth sense, it is a bit strange, you know...?'

'Yes, yes I do know…'

'So, he opens the door up and goes in. The room is dark, he goes for the lights but they have been disconnected…' Becky shifted in her chair.

'Anyway, it appears all of the family had shifted out and left the poor boy there in the corner of the living room under a blanket. The lad sadly passed. Beaten, battered, bruised. No longer with us.' Rod sat looking ruefully out of the pub window. Becky stared at him awaiting a punchline that never came.

'Is that the story, Rod?'

'Yeah. Pretty much.'

'Well, I hope you don't have any children as I'm not sure bedtime stories are your thing…'
'Oh, yeah! The reason I told you was because after that event, Charlie felt downtrodden and broken. Now I think it's natural for any man or woman to be disgusted by what he saw, and obviously affected. But Charlie, for all his skills and so on, he disappeared into a chasm. Not a literal one, a mefadori… a methadonical…… a….'
'Metaphorical?'
'That's it! Yeah, one of them, and Dave, me, and his other colleagues couldn't find him for a month. Turns out he had taken a little boat out onto the sea and just kept sailing. Came back when he was ready.'
'Yeah, but he has a baby to look after now…'
'Oh yeah, good point. My suggestion is that he is probably at home with her…'
'Yeah, but he won't open the door or answer his phone!'
'Then my suggestion would be to find a way in, to him. He's a man who has suffered great loss. What do you think may bring him back?'
Becky sat thinking.
Without Tara it was going to be virtually impossible to try and motivate her old partner…
'Hamartia… his fatal flaw… he is a terminal worrier, he becomes consumed by fear and darkness, he can't find his way out of it…'
'So, we need to bring him back to the light…'
'Well, yeah, I guess…'
'Rod, you are a genius!'
'Not the first time I have heard that, if I am honest…'
Becky looked bemused at the strange man in front of her.

'You know I have never been chatted up in such an odd yet endearing way, Rod.' She smiled. 'Are you going to buy me a drink?'

'Why, of course…' As Rod turned to the bar, the door slammed open and in walked one half of the McCarthy Brothers.

'Watcha Johnny. How are you?' The barman said, moving from Rod down to the front of the bar.

'On second thoughts, Rod, bugger that. Let's get out of here, eh?'

'My chariot awaits…'

20

'I can't be doing with any of those McCarthy pricks… they really wind me up…' Becky said, a little louder than she first intended.

Her voice reverberated around the dark, empty Folkestone street, as Rod stood impassive, walking by her side.

'Where to next?'

'You know Rod… I have had a shitty couple of weeks. Why don't we get a bottle or two and head back to mine?'

Becky looked over to Rod as his eyes widened at the invitation.

'Sure, that would be fine, Becky.'

'It's not an invitation to anything, Rod, you know? Just a chat with a… friend… I feel like I have known you for years…'

'I get that a lot too… the friendzone…'

'Hm. We'll see, Rod. We'll see.'

The pair walked towards the harbour, stopping at the off-licence on Tontine Street before heading back up Dover Road to Becky's flat that was opposite the fried chicken shop.

'So, Rod, you seem to like Charlie Stone quite a bit. How come you are not in contact anymore?'

'No real reason. Just the usual stuff, I guess. Men not keeping in contact, not… paying enough attention I suppose. Plus, we haven't got much in common. I'm into my old school drum n' bass and he likes… whatever he likes.'

'It's a shame you can't just text now and again. Maybe spend five minutes on a call?'

'Yeah, you're right. We should. I will try to make

more of an effort, I guess.'
'He gets down you know…'
'Yep, don't we all…'
'Oh, come on Rod! Mr Funny-man, approaching young ladies in pubs, don't tell me you get all glum too?' Rod looked up at Becky and their eyes met. She saw the sadness in them and realised the stupidity of her words.
'Everyone gets sad sometimes, Bex.'
Becky nodded, before leaning over and giving Rod a peck on the cheek.
'Still, don't get any ideas, matey.' She said opening the door to her flat and ushering him in.

Steve McCarthy found the little dirt track disconcerting as he slowly made his way to meet the wizard.
Another drop off, another new location. The wizard was nothing if not cautious.
He knew that he needed to drive very slowly and as such, he spent far too much time looking out of the window at the darkness and the solitude that lay in the countryside around him. It wasn't that he hated the countryside, he just preferred the business of town life.
As he got out of the car, he had to watch his step. The ground was uneven, he was unsure what he was stepping on.
Cow pat?
Thistle bush?
Or even worse, a grass snake or adder! He had been reading up on some of the delights one could come face to face with out here. He shivered, and then went to the backseat to pick up the small baby-sized

package that was there.
He had gotten quite used to handling babies. There was something about their warm little bodies and their need to snuggle that made Steve feel quite positive about himself.
This one was silent.
Sucking on his dummy, with his little green hat on and eyes closed.
In the distance, Johnny saw the flashing light of the wizard's handheld torch move slowly towards him.
Steve waited until the wizard was in view and he smiled at the old man.
'Steve,' he said softly.
'Hello. How are you?'
'Good, very good. How are you?'
'OK… yep.'
'How's that brother of yours?'
'Yeah fine. I mean… it's difficult, you know…'
'He wants to know what you are doing. With me, I mean.'
'Yeah,' Steve said softly, looking down at the ground.
'But I haven't told him anything, I promise.'
'I believe you, Steve. I believe you. But, it's why we must meet here. We can't take any risks
now.'
'I understand.'
'You know how important this work is.'
'I do. I want to keep going.' Steve said, almost desperately.
The wizard looked at him, then put his hand to Steve's face.
'We will try, Steve.'
He wasn't reassured.
'He wants to control you, your brother. He controls

everybody and everything, but he cannot control you. He doesn't like it. You understand?'
'Yep, he's always been the same…'
'No, but *do you understand?*' The wizard grabbed Steve's arm and pulled him closer to him, the baby clamped firmly to his shoulder with the other.
Steve looked deep into the wizard's bright, blue eyes.
'If he cannot control you Johnny, he will try and destroy you.'
The wizard let go and started walking back across the Kentish Marsh.

'Here Becky, I've got an idea.'
'OK...'
'Doesn't Charlie have an older daughter?'
'Yep, Maddie. Why?'
'Well, what is she doing now? Can't you get her to speak to her dad?'
Becky pondered Rod's solution.
Let the light in.
'That, Rod, is a very good idea! Let's find her and bring her to him.'
'Yeah, I'm not sure that I can...'
'Bollocks, Rod. You are coming too.'
'But, I...'
'No buts, Rod. He needs help.'
Rod looked at the beautiful lady in front of him and slowly nodded.
'OK. Let's do it.'

Charlie placed Ridley down in her cot, making sure she was wrapped fully in the cream blanket that Tara had bought for her a few weeks previously.
He found her dummy quickly and managed to place it

in her mouth before she began crying again. He watched her, so tiny, so helpless, yet with the ability to conquer his world in a matter of minutes.
He watched her eyes as they slowly moved around in her tiny head, rolling and rolling before her eyelids shut. He smiled at how punchdrunk a bottle of milk always made her. He remembered his beer on the side and picked it up, taking a swig. It had got a bit warm, so he decided to down it quickly and then start on the vodka and diet cokes.
He checked the time, 4.30pm.
He looked down again at Ridley who was gone now, in a happy land of nod.
Charlie descended the stairs and went to the kitchen cupboard that used to hold the cereals and bread.
It now helo 1.5 litres of vodka and a large bottle of diet coke.
He pulled them out from the cupboard before placing them on the side. He went to the freezer to grab some ice from the trays, but was irritated to find that he hadn't refilled them from last night.
He did it now and resigned himself to having at least one warm voddy and coke. Well maybe two.
He poured the drink, a thick two fingers of clear liquid.
He liked to be able to taste the alcohol, to know he was slipping off into his netherworld, sooner rather than later.
After grabbing the glass from the side, he walked back up the stairs and towards the PlayStation that was waiting on pause… *Tsushima Island, still yet to be conquered.*
He sat in bed and took up the controller, placing it in his lap.

The drawer was calling him as he took the game off pause and continued riding through the forests of southern Asia. His heartbeat sped up as he became excited. Bartering with himself… normally he waited until 6pm, but well… he could have a couple now, just to tide him over.

He paused the game again and opened the drawer, pulling out a small jar of cream-coloured pills.

He unscrewed the top and placed two pills in his hand, before scoffing them back, forcing them down with warm, strong vodka and diet coke.

He knew the pills would begin to kick in soon.

He smiled to himself and resumed his computer game.

21

Johnny McCarthy pulled up at the gates of the old facility on Dover Road.
The sound of his tyres grinding to a halt alerted one of the under-19s on guard, who looked directly through the slat in the door. Upon seeing Johnny's car, he opened the gate, as Johnny roared past him, nearly knocking the kid over in the process.
'Easy fam!' the kid said, as the car came to a sudden halt.
'What did you say?' Johnny barked, getting out from the car.
'Nothing, boss. Sorry, boss,' the kid said.
Johnny shot him a firm glance and realised he had bigger issues to attend to. He slammed his door and headed towards the fluorescent light of the main building.
Johnny realised that he had left his keycard at home, so went to the door and looked through the window.
He saw Doctor Smith through the glass and hammered his flat palm on the glass.
The doctor moved swiftly to the door and opened it fully. He entered and walked straight into the lab where Smith had been sifting through papers.
'Hi Mr McCarthy,' the doctor said tentatively.
'Doc. What's happening?'
'Well, erm… as I am sure you are aware, there has been a slight urm…'
'...fuck up, Rob?'
'Well, it's a…'
'Disaster?'
'No, no…'
'Why did I just get a call saying that another subject

has copped it? Burned from the inside out? How can this happen?'
'It's an experiment. There will be varying... *results.*'
'But, why are you letting these guys out, on the street? You know this will make the newspaper don't you? We saw another guy in agony down the harbour the other day...'
'There, um, simply isn't the space for the amount of test subjects coming in. Look, I only have the cells along here... so after the two week period, we have to let the initial ones go.'
'Well don't let them go! Keep them here! Double them up if you have to...'
'We are already...'
'Well get rid of them here, we can't have the publicity...'
'I am afraid that... I mean... we are not *murderers...*'
Johnny smirked and gave the doctor a wry smile.
'This is on you, old man. People are beginning to ask questions... if there are anymore fuck-ups, my brother and I will tear your fucking head off.'
The doctor looked down at the floor and nodded.
'Sorry, Mr McCarthy, it won't happen again.'
'Your right it won't!'
The doctor recoiled in fear at the young man lurching across the lab towards him.
Steve laughed at the cowardice of the doctor, before turning on his heel and heading back to the door.
The doctor waited for the door to slam behind Mr McCarthy, before taking a deep breath and smiling to himself.
He picked up the phone.
'Yessir. Hello. Smith, yes. In relation to our earlier

discussion, he bought it. Yes, hook, line and sinker. That's right. OK, no problem. I will. I understand. Thank you, sir. Thank you.'

Smith put the phone down and went towards the cells beyond the laboratory.

He turned to check that the labs at the front were entirely empty before locking the door behind him.

He went along the corridor and looked at the empty cells before getting out his keycard and opening the cell furthest on the right. He checked his surroundings just to make sure, before entering and locking the door behind him again.

He took a deep breath and moved to the far end of the cell which again, was empty.

He stood at the far wall of the cell, and looked up at it, running his hands upon the wall.

At around eye level, he felt a groove in the flat, coldness of the metal wall.

He pressed the button and held it down for two seconds, stepping back.

There was a clicking sound before Doctor Smith pushed firmly in the centre of the wall, revealing a hidden door that he slid open slowly.

Doctor Smith took one last check of the locked cell, before sliding the door closed behind him and heading into the darkness in front of him.

22

Charlie noticed that he wasn't really focused anymore on the storyline of the game.
His eyes were blurring occasionally, as he explored the beautiful landscapes of Tsushima Island.
He had forgotten how many pills he had taken now, and his fourth drink was almost empty. Luckily, he had ice now and on his last visit to the kitchen, found a small lemon that he had sliced and was using in his drink, to pretend there was some class left to his behaviour.
He put the controller down and paused his game. The time popped up on the screen, 7.32pm.
He downed the last little bit of drink before jumping from the bed to grab a refill, he was a bit woozy from the booze and pills, falling into the wall a little on his way into Ridley's room.
She was fine, still sleeping like a baby, but he decided to get her a bottle of milk as he predicted she would wake within the next half hour.
As he sprinted down the stairs and turned for the kitchen, there was a loud knock at the front door.
Charlie froze.
He was in full view of the frosted glass panel on the main part of the door. However, he snuck quietly down to the bottom step and around into the sanctuary of the kitchen, or so he thought.
'Uhm, Charlie, we can see you moving in there,' Becky shouted through the door.
Charlie stayed stock still behind the cover of the wall, hoping, praying that she would go away.
'Come on, Charlie. Open the door. We just want to talk to you.' She continued.

We? *We?*

Who else did Becky have with her? Maybe Jacko... maybe... no... as if...

From behind the door, Becky nudged Rod in the ribs to get him to say something.

'Ahem, err Detective... I mean... uh, Charlie... bloody hell, Charlie, it's me Rod... it's good to see you... I mean... you know what I mean...'

Rod coughed and Becky looked derisorily at him.

Charlie smiled to himself. He missed Rod... he missed people... *no Charlie, don't be weak, stay in the comfort of what you know...*

'Charlie, come on!' Becky said, becoming frustrated.

There was a small groan from upstairs, that turned into a whimper and then into a wail.

The milk, the bloody milk!

Charlie slipped back up the stairs as quietly as he could, deciding it was wiser to grab the baby before heading back down to make the milk for her, that way she would be comforted.

He went in and picked up the small, warm bundle from the cot before heading back downstairs as quietly as he could.

He didn't look, but he could tell there were bodies still behind his front door.

'Dad. Dad!' came a girl's voice and once again, Charlie froze.

A feeling of warmth flooded through the numbness and he turned and slowly made his way to the front door.

He opened it slowly and was greeted by the small frame of his daughter, Maddie.

She ran at him and hugged him, he wobbled slightly, but soon regained his composure. There he was, in a

warm embrace with his daughters.
'Dad, you smell. Sorry, but you do. Why don't you go take a shower?'
Yeah, we can feed Ridley.' Becky added.
'Your mum said you weren't to come here anymore, Mad.' Charlie said huskily.
'Yeah well, what she doesn't know, eh?'
'Are those sweatpants, Charlie? Grubby *sweatpants?* I don't think I have ever seen you in… is the washing machine actually working? Look at the state of you…' Becky said, moving towards her old partner and pulling him in for a brief hug.
'Gosh… back on the sauce, eh?' she said softly to him.
'All right, I got it, I'll take a shower, jeez! The baby milk is in the second cupboard, not the first.' he said as he stomped upstairs.
Becky took Ridley from Maddie and headed to the kitchen.
'He is black, but he is coming back. Little elements of green and orange. But we still have someway to go,' Maddie said, into the air.
Rod stared confused.
'Yeah dudette, totally trippy.'
Charlie went and turned the shower on, leaving it to warm up and with a heavy sigh turned off the PlayStation in the bedroom.

Charlie headed back downstairs and into the front room, tentatively. The three of them were sitting there, Ridley was in the downstairs cot, asleep again.
It felt a little like an intervention, though obviously that was not the purpose of the visit.
'Good to see you, Charlie, looking a bit more like it

now!' she smiled encouragingly.
'It's been a rough few weeks…'
'Oh, I didn't mean, you know…'
'It's OK, Bex…'
'Yeah, I mean, we just worried about you…'
'I know. But I was no good. Good to see you, Rod. What have you been up to?'
'Oh, you know. Ducking, diving. The usual stuff.'
'Or drinking and playing pool in the local pub!' Becky remarked.
'Yeah, well whatever… Charlie, you are… you know…'
'Spit it out, Rod!' Maddie laughed.
'Well, everyone thinks you are a hero at the nick…'
'Yeah, good one, Rod.'
'No, I mean it Char, you are like… Ultimate Warrior or something. They are gutted you left the force…'
'Trust me, I am not going back.'
'No, that's not what I meant. I just wanted you to know what you did for… you know what I mean…'
'Thanks, Rod.'
Becky looked at Rod smiling.
'So, Mad. How are you?' Charlie asked.
'I'm good, dad. Was worried about you but good to see you are OK. I mean, we had to open a few windows and Becky has had to do a bit of tidying… but generally…you seem… all right.'
'Listen, I'm sorry I haven't been around. I mean, Maddie, I have been trying to call…'
'Yeah, my mum wouldn't let…'
'Don't worry, it's OK, you are here now… and I just couldn't make sense of it and I just needed to be on my own…'
'You blame yourself for what happened, dad. You

always do…' Maddie said, staring straight at her father.
The other two sat awkwardly, Becky wondering whether to soften the blow of Maddie's harsh words.
'Yeah…'
'But, it's not your fault. Trust me, I know.'
'I appreciate it, Mad, but…'
'No, I mean it. All of the things you blame yourself for. It's normal. Everyone feels bad and blames themselves, but it doesn't mean it's always their fault.'
'I should have protected Tara…'
'Tara wanted to be with you, Charlie. Dave wanted to be with you, at your side, to help you. And that's why we are here too. OK?' Becky added.
Charlie's eyes filled with tears, he felt appalling. The vodka and drugs coursing through his veins. His self-pity, the vacuum of darkness he had fallen into, he wanted to erase it all.
Becky came to him and kneeled in front of him as he wept. She held him and kissed his face tenderly.
'So, uhm, seen that new Spiderman film, Maddie?' Rod asked awkwardly across the room.
'Yes, it's absolutely sick!' she returned.
Becky and Charlie took the hint and separated.
'Sorry.' Charlie said to the room.
'Leave it out, dad. We got some baddies to catch.'
Charlie nodded and summoned his daughter to him. After grabbing her in a bear hug that was a little too tight, he nodded.
'Yes, I think you are right.'
'Erm, hey… uh, Charlie… I am no expert here but can you have a look at Ridley?' Becky said.
Charlie stood up quickly and felt a little woozy still

from the pills he took earlier, the beauty of vodka was that it still made him feel sharper than he would, had he been guzzling beer or red wine.

Ridley had a rash across her face that was bright red.

Looking at the rest of her body after taking off her baby grow, it had spread all the way down her back.

'Mad, can you grab me a thermometer from the first aid drawer, please?'

Charlie was trying to remain calm in the face of another life-altering disaster.

He picked the baby up. She felt limp and lifeless.

Charlie's breathing sped up as Maddie passed him the thermometer.

He placed it under her arm and waited.

'Erm, I think I'm going to go now...' Rod said quietly to Becky, who nodded her approval, his work here was largely done and this was a little bit above and beyond, despite his generally good intentions.

Charlie was too transfixed on the small plastic length to notice anything else.

The wait seemed to take forever as Rod saw himself out, but eventually the double beep broke the silence.

Forty-two degrees.

'We have to go to the hospital. Now.'

23

Steve McCarthy was avoiding his brother's calls.
As he drove from the facility, he kept watching his phone glow blue with Johnny's number and then disappear.
This was the thirteenth time.
The man was relentless, and Steve knew he would have to answer to him some time soon, but currently he was not in the mood for further argument and aggression.
The phone glowed once more, but this time it was a number he recognised that was not his brother.
He answered immediately.
'Hey!'
'Hi, Steve, how are you?' The wizard asked.
'Oh, same old, same old.'
'That brother of yours again?'
'Yeah, something like that.'
'Remember what I said to you, he wants to control…'
'...I know, I get it. I just need some time, some headspace to be able to talk to him again. You know what he is like.'
'Hm. Well, if you have time, I have… one last assignment…'
'Oh, really? You… I thought you said that it was over?'
'I did, but there was a small issue, a tragedy even, something unavoidable. As such there is space for one more…'
'OK. OK, yes definitely. I will get straight on it.'
'That would be good. And thanks.'
'I'll call you later tonight, when it's done.'

The wizard hung up the phone and Steve felt that glorious glow of purpose, a feeling that he mattered again.
He turned the car around and headed home to get changed.

'It will be OK, Charlie. Babies are like… completely the priority in hospital, that's why she has gone straight in, top of the list, you know?'
Charlie's knee was jigging up and down, which kept the baby Ridley rocking in his arms. He listened closely for her breath that was going quickly, a little too quickly.
'Mr Stone?'
Charlie nodded to the woman in a white coat.
'This way.'
'I'll stay here with Maddie, OK?' Becky said.
Charlie nodded again and followed the lady into one of the rooms. The doctor asked Charlie to lay the baby in a small plastic cot.
There was a flurry of activity.
Nurses walked in, doctors walked out.
Doors opened and closed.
Charlie tried to sense the tone.
Was there panic?
How was the doctor's voice?
Is she calm, or was it just a front?

Steve McCarthy pulled up to the hospital and parked in the lay by out front.
He had never been told off, or got a ticket, despite the fact he left the car there regularly. Perhaps there was no-one on security to check, or perhaps they made so much money from the people legitimately parking in

the car park, that they didn't worry.
Still, Steve didn't want to take long.
Although he enjoyed the process of what he was doing, he didn't enjoy being in the hospital.
The flourescent lights.
The long, drawn faces.
The stench of death.
No, he would be quick, in and out.
He had already phoned ahead and told his contact that he would be arriving, so that he didn't have the same debacle as last time, getting into the maternity ward.
As he approached the building, he felt his phone buzz in his pocket.

Little girl, few months, A and E room 3.

Hm.
It certainly was less conspicuous in A and E. More bodies floating, rushing. He could just blend in and blend out with his prize.
But, A and E? What was wrong with the kid?
He decided to mooch over and see what was going on anyway, just in case.
He looked about moving in and out of sick patients and rushing doctors, until he found the room.
He looked in and saw a doctor tapping away furiously at a computer in the corner. In front of him lay a small, plastic cot, with a calm, sleeping baby.
She looked so cute, all wrapped up there… Steve moved silently into the room and stood over Ridley.
He looked at the doctor who was facing her computer, oblivious to his presence. Either way, one look at his pistol and she would soon shut up, he was sure.
He looked down again at the baby, about to make his

move.

'Are you all right there, mate?' a voice spoke from behind him.

'All right, yeah. Just trying to find my missus and our kid, she is up here somewhere, but... no bloody reception.'

Steve turned around and was face to face with Charlie Stone.

'I know you. One of the McCarthy boys. I have seen you up here with babies before. What are you up to?'

'Sir, you should not be in here...' the doctor said removing her glasses.

'Yeah, like I said. My baby, I have just had a daughter...'

'Yeah? Well, why were you about to grab *my daughter*, eh?' Charlie said, moving towards him.

'Both of you shouldn't really be in here, we are trying to stabilise the patient...'

'Relax, Charlie. It's just a case of mistaken identity. I promise you.'

Charlie stood silent. Watchful, taking in the information. He didn't believe this joker for one minute, but his priority was keeping his daughter away from harm. He thought about Johnny McCarthy what better way to attain revenge than to twar his little brother limb from limb...

'All right, a case of mistaken identity, I guess. Off you go.' Charlie said, thinking better of it.

'I'm sorry your daughter is in here, Charlie. Is she OK?'

'Listen, stop calling me Charlie. I'm not your mate.'

Steve looked deflated and nodded, taking his leave from the scene.

Charlie followed him out and picked up his phone.

'Becky, where are you?'
'Where I left you…'
'Good. Steve McCarthy. He's headed your way. Sandy coloured jacket...'
'Yep, got him.' Becky whispered into the phone, as Steve walked by.
'Tail him. He is up to something. I found him standing over Ridley.'
'Wait, what? Jesus! Is she OK?' Becky asked.
'I think so. It's to do with the exomphalos. She may need a procedure, but nothing serious, or invasive.'
'Oh, that's good. Charlie, got some bad news.'
'Right…'
'Yeah, Jo tracked Maddie's phone and found where she was. She has just come to get her.'
'Tracked her phone?'
'Yep. Perhaps she learnt a few things from your marriage, huh? Either way, Maddie is gone. She said to say goodbye. She loves you.'
'OK. Well, thanks for watching her, Bex. And for dealing with the ex.'
'Yeah, I can see why you got divorced. Anyway, leave me to it, I'm gonna find out what Mr McCarthy is up to.'
'Nice one.'
Charlie put the phone down and went back into room three.
'Everything OK?'
'Yes, perhaps you should wait in here. I have just called the specialist who is en-route to see… Ridley.'
'Yes, maybe that might be best.'

Becky made her way out of the building and watched Steve McCarthy get into his car.

She turned right out of the exit and crossed the pedestrian crossing towards the car park. In her bag, she had a beanie hat and a scarf which she put on as soon as she was out of sight, whilst keeping an eye on the blue car that McCarthy was in.
He hadn't turned the engine on, so Becky was in no hurry to get to her vehicle. She tried to see what he was doing, but it was difficult from this distance. She loitered around the payment machine, until McCarthy opened his car door and got out. He stuffed his hands in his jacket pocket after shutting the door and moved back inside the building with intent. Purpose.
Becky crossed the road and followed through the sliding doors and watched her prey walk up the main corridor through the hospital building.
She stayed a decent distance away but kept him firmly in her sights. He moved quickly, as if he knew where he was going, he turned the corner at the end of the corridor and headed towards the Folkestone and Maternity Wards.
Becky knew she had to be careful. If she turned the corner she would be in full view, so she waited at the corner for a wheelchair patient to move around her, before taking a peek at the corridor.
McCarthy was nowhere to be seen causing Becky to panic, so she moved swiftly along.
She looked into the Maternity Ward as she passed and saw a flash of his sandy jacket.
She went to push the door open, but was too late, it had locked behind him.
She decided to stay outside and wait for him to return. She had no reason to be on the ward and thought it would be too conspicuous for her to think of some elaborate excuse.

There was an outside chance that he would find an alternative exit and she would lose him. But what were the odds of that happening? Or indeed, of there being another exit from the ward?
She stood outside and waited, hoping that no-one would pass her and she wouldn't have to explain what she was doing.
It was in these situations she wished for Charlie, and the way he was able to always think of a brilliant excuse or line to smooth these awkward moments.
She decided to get her phone out and pretend to be texting. The plan worked, and she did notice a few unread texts, one from Rod and two from Maddie, who had clearly saved her number. She smiled.

Hey, Becky thanks for finding me. I was worried about dad.

If anything happens, I want to come and help. Let me know. Mad x

Becky nodded silent approval. She then skipped to Rod's WhatsApp.

Fancy going for a cheeky dinner sometime?

Becky snorted, but held back her laughter.
Did she want to go for a dinner? With Rod? God knows, she thought to herself.
She looked up, perplexed, and noticed the thick set frame of Steve McCarthy speed past her, with a small, blankety bundle in his arms.
She looked back down at her phone and then put it to her ear to pretend to make a call.

She bounced from foot to foot as McCarthy made his way past her and back towards the open-plan foyer of the hospital.
She needed to time it well or she would lose him. He would be in his car and off within minutes… maybe even seconds.
She needed to get out without being noticed, pay for her parking, and get through the barrier.
Bugger!
She trod lightly, but speedily through the hospital and out of the main door.
She took a cursory glance to her left and saw that McCarthy was having some difficulty placing the bundle into his car seat.
She saw that the queue for the parking meter was two people deep. She waited with one eye on the car. McCarthy was still trying to strap the baby in, but it wouldn't take him long and then he would be off.
'Excuse me, I'm really sorry but can I push in front quickly? I am an off-duty police officer…'
The old lady at the front of the queue looked angrily at Becky.
'Where's your badge, love?'
Becky looked forlorn, but went to her bag to grab… well, she didn't know what.
'I'm only jesting, sweetheart. Of course you can go!' the lady chortled.
'Oh, goodness…. Thankyou!'
Becky inserted her ticket and paid in lightning quick time. The blue car in the drop-off bay was pulling away gently.
Becky sprinted to the car, as she watched McCarthy's car speed up and move towards the mini-roundabout and past the private hospital.

Becky got in and started her engine, as the car turned left and onto the bypass towards the Crooksfoot roundabout.
Becky sped to the exit and rammed her ticket in the slot. The barrier took an age to rise, and she toyed with smashing through it, but thought better of it. If she had to chase a suspect, it would be better to do it in a working car, that is for sure.
Her phone rang, Charlie Stone.
'Bad timing, Charlie.' Becky said aloud, before speeding right and then left at the mini-roundabout, causing two cars to emergency stop to a chorus of horns.
At the next set of traffic lights, she could see a blue car heading towards Badmunstereifel Road. She jumped the lights again and was now sitting twenty metres or so away from Steve McCarthy's car.
She felt a real sense of achievement and excitement. *This was real work.*
Her phone rang again.
'Hi, Charlie,' she said.
'How is it going?'
'Well, it has been tricky, but I still have him clocked. I'm following him in the car now.'
'Excellent, Bex. Excellent. Stay on him. It may get a bit dark. God knows what he is doing with these babies… but just find out where he is going and I will take it from there.'
'I can handle it, Charlie!'
'Sorry, Bex. You know what I mean… I don't want to sound…'
'Patronising! That's how you sound. I can do stuff you know, this little feeble woman…'
'Come on, you know that's not what I… I just don't

want… I think it could get grim, Becky.'
'Listen, I got to go. Talk to you later.'
Becky put the phone down and followed the blue car along the dual carriageway, towards the A2070.
She knew Charlie meant well, but part of her really wanted to prove something to him. That she was capable. She didn't have the plaudits and the badges and the headlines that Charlie bloody Stone did, but she could still do things properly.
The cars headed on to the A2070 and Becky knew she was able to drop further back to ensure that McCarthy didn't suspect he was being followed.

Steve McCarthy picked up the phone and dialled his last called number as the bundle in the back screamed blue murder.
'Hi, I am en route, five minutes away.'
'OK, Steve. Sounds like I will need milk. See you there.'
McCarthy felt a searing sadness when the babies cried. He wanted to help them, to nurture them. To make them feel secure and happy.
But he was merely a middleman.
He pressed his foot harder onto the accelerator pedal.

24

'Hi mum,' Charlie said, relieved, as she came bustling into the waiting area at the William Harvey Hospital.

'How is she?'

'Well, I think she is going to be OK. Do you remember she had that issue with the vital organs growing on the outside, in utero…'

'...Exomphalus?'

'Yes, that…'

'Yes?'

'Well, they think it is a complication to do with it, but she is fine at the moment. She is on a drip, which is not nice, but she is resting. The specialist is coming any minute to see whether she needs to have an operation… or what the next steps are…'

'Right.' Charlie's mum looked solemn. She tried to keep a calm, assertive presence, but Charlie could tell that she was concerned… scared, even.

As was Charlie, of course.

He was still numb and grieving his wife, the thought of losing… it didn't bear thinking about.

'Do you want to get off then? I'll hold the fort here. Get some rest. Take your mind off it…'

His mum said hopefully. Charlie gave a wry smile.

'I know. But, at least you could try.'

'Yes, I will. Thanks mum.'

Charlie could feel tears form in his eyes as he moved forward and hugged his mother. He didn't want to let her go. He wanted to stay in the embrace forever and not come back to this horrible, brutal reality.

He wanted to rewind twenty-five years and start again.

Without all the mess-ups.
His mother let him go.
'It will be OK, Charlie.'
His mum was bleary-eyed too.
Charlie got up from the chair and walked outside of the waiting room and into the cool, evening air.
He checked his phone and saw that Becky had sent him some coordinates. This was good, if he was working, then he wasn't thinking about Tara or Ridley.
He tapped the coordinates into Google Maps and went to find his car.
It was dusk as Charlie left Willesborough and began travelling to Becky's location. Now he had a moment to collect himself, his hangover was beginning to set in firmly. He felt like an idiot. Masking his shame and his grief with gallons of booze and prescription pills. He took a deep breath and resolved to turn it around, for Maddie, for Ridley.
As he pulled up next to Becky's car and got out, the light orange glow of sunset fell over the marshes.
The river Rother trickled gently to their left, and there was the occasional sound of vehicles speeding towards their destinations behind them.
'You OK?' Charlie said as he hopped into Becky's passenger seat. He noticed that smell. Her smell. Fruity, crisp, feminine.
He looked at Becky, surprised.
She was wide-eyed and staring at him. They both smiled.
'Yeah, I'm OK. How is Ridley?'
'She's going to be… I think… I mean I don't know, I left her there with my mother. The specialist is going to see her.'

'Jesus, Charlie. Don't you want to be there? I mean, I'm glad you are here, but…'
'There's nothing I can do. She is stable and sleeping. The specialist could be hours, you know what it's like…'
'True… it's best you're distracted actually, and helping me.' she said supportively.
'So, where is he? Where's the baby?'
'He headed with the bundle up to that point…' Becky indicated into the distance with her hand. Do you see that stone wall?'
Charlie squinted, but it was all a blur.
'Wait there.'
Charlie dived out of the car and grabbed his utility bag from the boot of his car.
He got back in and fished out two pairs of binoculars from the bag.
Becky nodded and realised that maybe she needed to invest in her own items for the job.
Through the lenses they could see Steve McCarthy facing away from them, talking to a man in what appeared to be a long, white robe.
'What is that about? Fancy dress?' Becky joked.
'Could be some kind've cult. Nothing I've seen before. Don't recognise the guy…'
Becky swallowed hard. The crashing realisation of all that Charlie had seen and experienced in the past few years made her feel… well… insignificant.
'So, partner. How shall we play this?' Charlie said softly.
Becky smiled, it was as if he knew how she was feeling at times, like a strange synergy was growing between them.
'He's going to hand the baby over, to the weird old

KKK guy, then McCarthy will head back this way. We are going to need to scarper as his car is just up ahead. I think if we move this car to get a better vantage point, then we can follow the robey guy and the baby, without getting spotted by McCarthy.'
Becky shot a glance at Charlie, who smiled.
'Excellent plan, Batman. Let's get moving, eh?'
Becky started the car and followed the country road which took them around eighty metres due east of the pair who were still talking in the middle of the marsh.

'This is the last one for the foreseeable future, Stephen.' The wizard spoke.
'Hm. You said that last time.'
'I mean it this time. There was a problem as I told you, but really now this is the last time.'
'For good?'
'We shall see.'
'It's just…'
'I know, Stephen. I know. But you have your path, and one way or another, it needs to be cleared. Here hand him over.'
'Her…'
'Her? OK. OK.'
The wizard took the bundle and shifted the blanket to one side. He took out a small bottle of white liquid and gently placed it in the child's mouth.
'Are you OK? The wizard asked.
'So, so. You know.'
'And him?'
'He's the same as he always is. I can't… I'm trying to make a difference, but I can't…'
'He is a force of nature, Steve.'

Johnny's phone buzzed in his pocket. He picked it out and showed the phone to the wizard, who nodded.
'Call him. Try and resolve it. He's your brother. I need to head back. We will speak soon.'
'Can I… um…?'
The wizard turned back and looked at Steve.
'Not yet. I'm sorry, it's too volatile…'
'You mean *he's* too volatile…'
The wizard smiled at Stephen's forlorn figure.
'Soon, Stephen. I promise.'

'Right, that's McCarthy heading back now. Let's stop and keep an eye on Gandalf here and where he takes the kid.' Charlie said, raising his binoculars to his eyes.
'He's heading directly across the fields… where does he think he's going?'
'He must have a vehicle stashed somewhere…'
'Or maybe… a horse?'
'What, Charlie? You think he is going to take the kid on a bloody horse?'
'God knows, but there is nowhere around unless he is going to walk… what… all the way to Old Romney?'
'That's a mile and a half. He can't do, surely?'
'Wait a minute, he's stopped.'
'What is he doing?'
'He's looking around… he's, oh shit, he's looking this way… duck down a minute…'
'He can't see us from there…'
'Wait…seriously! Duck down, just in case!' Charlie repeated.
They both did, waited a moment, before Charlie placed the binoculars back on his eyes.

'Check this out…'
'You are kidding me… the magic man has disappeared?'
'Unless you can see him? I can't. Literally he has gone. Bollocks!'

'Johnny…' Steve said, answering his phone.
'Oh, dear brother of mine… I have been trying to reach you? Where have you been…'
'Have you been drinking, Johnny?'
'Well, what the fuck does it matter?'
'It doesn't, I guess. Look, let's have a chat, yeah?'
'Yes, we need that, little bro. We need a little sort out. Where are you?'
'Oh, um just outside of Ashford. You?'
'Dover.'
'You *have* been drinking…'
'Fuck off, will you? Meet you at Folkestone then. Facility. Half an hour. We can talk it out, yeah?'
'That would be good, Johnny. I don't want to argue. All right?'
'It would be good to sort some stuff out. See you, Steve.'

25

'It's too dangerous to go together, Becky.'
'Well… why don't you head off then?'
'Oh, come on Bex… I'm all for women's lib, but I am not sending you in there, especially given… you know… what happened at the facility.'
'Charlie, don't…'
'No, Becky. I let you down. It's my thing. It's what I do. Besides I…'
Charlie trailed off, but Becky knew where he was going. He needed a distraction. He needed to help. His wife had been killed, his baby was struggling for life in hospital. What was he going to do, go home and put Netflix on?
'I get it. You go. I'll get off. Shall I check in with your mum at the hospital?'
'You don't have to,' Charlie said softly.
'Good luck, buddy. I'm here if you need me.' Becky said, leaning in to give him a kiss, before Charlie got out of the car.
'Thanks, Bex. For everything.' he said solemnly.
'It's OK, old man. I'll see you soon.' she smiled her big friendly smile at him before starting the engine.
Charlie shut the door and took a deep breath.
He squashed the feelings of vulnerability and fear that had risen up inside him, as Becky put her car into first gear and slowly pulled away. How many times had he gone into dangerous situations on his own?
Hundreds.
Yet here and now, he wanted Becky to stay.
She provided a warm comfort, she understood him and she cared. She loved him unconditionally. Yet it wasn't physical… at least that's what Charlie

believed.
There was also her great skill as a detective and her feistiness, her tenacity, her desire to not give in. He loved that about her.
He watched her car signal right in the distance and disappear into the vast grey nothingness of the A2070.
He was on his own.
No Dave.
No Tara.
No Bex.
What was the plan?
He had to find the kid and try to save him. Logic taught him that the man in the white robe went into an underground hatch, invisible from here.
Given the trajectory, that underground hatch would lead directly east… which would lead somewhere near… nowhere.
An empty field.
Right, Charlie walked towards where 'the disappearing' occurred. The light was gone and he was not hopeful in the vast oasis of the marsh that he would find anything that he was looking for, especially in the dark.
He needed to find another way in.
He pulled out his phone and opened Google Maps. The nearest place of any interest in the vicinity was an old abandoned farm called Notwells.
Charlie had no other bright ideas, despite searching like a needle in a haystack for an opening in the grassy marsh, that may not even be there, so jogged back to the car and headed towards the coordinates of the farm.

When Charlie arrived at Notwells, it appeared largely deserted.
He drove towards two large green gates, down a short little lane, which was muddy and bumpy in equal measure.
He jumped out of the car and looked through the small hole just underneath the padlock that wrenched the two doors together.
There were a number of old aircraft hangers, some with rusty old machinery such as tractors and other farming paraphernalia. More pertinently, the area seemed quiet, there was no sign of life.
Charlie looked for a way to jump the fence but it was over 2.5 metres high. He walked around to the side of the fence and followed the perimeter of it. He realised now, the sheer size and scale of the farm, it seemed far too big to be hiding out here in the middle of nowhere. He continued to walk, and noticed that the terrain had become far more 'woody.' There were overhanging trees, and his footing was becoming trickier, as he moved over tree roots, branches and slippery leaves to stay alongside the wall. Night time in the country was unnervingly dark, and brought with it a chill to the air, causing Charlie's breath to cloud up in little twists of mist in front of his face.
He pulled out his phone to use the torchlight held within it, and noticed that he had no texts and no notifications, largely due to the fact that he had zero reception.
He continued to walk in the dark, keeping the flashlight firmly on his footing and a metre or so ahead of him.
There was a significant drop down before him, at least a metre and a half. The large fence seemed to

curve down to accommodate this, however Charlie was going to have to make a precarious leap if he was to continue on his current route.
He made sure his footing was secure and jumped, rolling along the soft carpet of leaves that covered the hard ground. Getting to his feet, he took a look around with his torch and noticed something quite peculiar, something he very much didn't expect to see in an old industrial facility somewhere in the Romney Marsh.
Covered by overhanging brambles, Charlie saw a brown wooden door with an old-fashioned door knocker upon it.
It appeared to lead either into or under Notwells farm, so Charlie moved tentatively towards it.

26

Steve pulled into the facility on Dover Road to find that his brother's car was already there, parked to the side.

He parked behind it and got out.

'Hello brother,' came a voice in the darkness.

Steve looked around but couldn't see Johnny anywhere.

'Can we turn the courtyard lights on? I can't see fuck all.'

'Sure thing.'

With that the courtyard was bathed in light, and Steve was greeted by a wall of under-19's, staring at him through their black balaclavas.

'All right, lads…' Steve started, before realising that something was terribly wrong here.

They didn't move but stood stock still, as he walked into the centre of the courtyard.

'What do you want, Johnny?' he shouted.

'A brother, boy. A family. But what have I got? I got *you!*'

Steve made his way through the band of underage misfits and came into view. He was wearing a long, black trenchcoat and black boots, and he moved slowly and certainly towards his brother.

His eyes were wide and steely.

'Listen, Johnny. Whatever you think the matter is, we can resolve it…'

'Not this time.'

Johnny made a move towards his brother and feigned to hit him with his left, before cracking his jaw with a sharp right hook.

Steve was staggered but remained on his feet.

'Listen, I ain't fighting you. You are tougher than me. You are a better fighter than…'
The second crack caught him harder as he fell to the floor.
'Yeah boi!'
'Finish it fam!'
'Get him bro!'
Came the shouts from the under -19's, baying for blood.
'What have I done? I'm your blood, Johnny… we grew up together! I fucking looked after you!'
Johnny chuckled. 'Yeah, yeah maybe. But what about now? You looking after me now?'
'Yes, I… I am doing what you want… I… we look after *each other…*'
There was another crack, this time to Steve's midriff and the air escaped his body like a ghost, disappearing into the air. His legs felt light and he dropped to his knees, as Johnny leaned into him and spoke in his ear.
'I know about the wizard. I know who he is.'
'Wait… what?'
'I also know you are a fucking faggot, Stevie. My own brother.'
'Jesus, Johnny… come on…'
'You betrayed me. My own family.'
'It was for your own good, Johnny. To protect you.'
'I don't need either you or him now. Lads.'
Johnny walked back through the crowd, as the gang surrounded Steve McCarthy and brought his life to a painful and bitter end.

Charlie turned the knocker to the left and pulled the door.

He was surprised to find it opened immediately and revealed a tunnel, dimly lit by electric lights that trailed along its descent.
He walked through the tunnel as it curved around, delving deeper and deeper underground.
The lights provided a warm, ethereal glow, so Charlie placed his phone back in his pocket.
The tunnel began to climb uphill, towards another wooden door.
He continued apace, beginning to feel somewhat claustrophobic. He got to the end to find that this door was locked. He pushed hard against it, but it was to no avail. He started to panic, being underground and worried now that the door at the end might be locked, that this might be some elaborate trap.
He went for his phone. No reception still.
Charlie was torn.
Did he head back?
Back to safety?
Return tomorrow in the light with his partner?
But what about the baby? What might happen to the little blankety bundle?
Charlie decided that he needed to get through the door, that this needed to be done tonight.
He pushed hard at the wooden door and the frame. He could certainly break through, but at what cost? Who would be waiting on the other side? Whatever is happening here, they didn't want to be found. This... well not entirely elaborate... but certainly a hidden entry to... *what?*
What was behind the door?
Charlie needed to know and let his anger flow, kicking it with all of his might. The thud reverberated through the tunnel. It was giving slowly, he continued

to boot and then to throw his body at the door.
One last push and the door gave way as Charlie fell through and onto the ground in front of him.

'Is he dead?'
'Yeah, blood. He ain't breathing.'
'Sick, right bring him to the labs. Guv'nor wants his body kept.'
'Aight, fam.'
The boys picked up Steve McCarthy's lifeless body and carried it towards the laboratory. Johnny McCarthy was in the main room with Doctor Robert Smith.
'Listen, Johnny. I understand, he is your brother, but the rules are the rules.' Smith said.
Johnny was sniffling, his head hung. Bereft.
'Lay him there. That's right. Good. Now fuck off. He just… he's my brother…'
'I know, but he betrayed us. He betrayed you. You know the rules.'
Johnny burst into floods of tears.
'He will get a proper burial, OK?'
Johnny nodded, but could not stop himself from weeping.

Charlie looked at the ground. He pushed himself up with his hands and noticed lush, green grass between his fingers.
As he got to his feet, he noticed that in front of him were a series of cloth-covered yurts and in the distance, there were some low-level wooden and brick buildings that were somewhat larger.
Surrounding him, were a number of beautiful, lush trees. Trees that had been pruned, manicured…

looked after. Trees that had a variety of different fruit growing. Apples, pears, plums…
There were decorative arches that were twinkling with fairy lights that seemed to lead somewhere just out of view.
Charlie checked his surroundings, and could see that there was no-one around, despite this place clearly being inhabited by someone… some group of people.
He continued walking through the arches before turning a corner and finding himself in a courtyard. It was quite beautiful, a fountain spraying foamy water sat in the centre. Around the sides were lodges and huts, surrounded by greenery, flowers and plant life.
'You have made it,' a voice came from behind him.
Charlie turned in panic, then saw the wizard standing before him. His white robe, his slow walk, made him seem holy, somewhat ethereal.
'What… What is this place?' Charlie asked.
'It's where you belong, Charlie. You found us.'
'Where is the kid? The baby? What the hell are you doing with the babies?' Charlie shouted.
The wizard just smiled.
'Follow me.'

Charlie was confused to say the least.
He knew that he was here to fight crime, to save the children. He was pent up with rage and fury. But yet, there was a serenity to this scene that made him second guess himself. Either way, he had no option but to follow the wizard for now.
'I understand your confusion, Charlie. You are wondering why a local gangster is stealing babies from a hospital…'
'What is this place?'

'It would make sense, for this to be some... unpleasant criminal activity to you...'
'Is this like a cult? I know about Charlie Manson, pal. In five minutes, I can have back up and...'
'To you in your world, this makes no sense...'
Charlie got out his phone; unsurprisingly he had no reception.
'Take it easy, Charlie. Relax.'
The wizard led Charlie to a wooden lodge that appeared from the outside rather warm and homely.
'Be quiet, Charlie. We don't want anyone to wake up.'
The wizard slowly opened the door and Charlie followed him inside. The large room was dark, but there were dim lights at either end. The wizard went to a light switch and slowly increased the glow in the room.
'Oh, wow...'
The room was long and rectangular in shape, decorated in light blues and pinks. There was a rainbow at one end surrounded by fluffy white clouds. The mural stretched across the back wall and turned into a glorious country scene: cows, pigs and sheep.
The sides walls were painted too; one side in blue with a moon. It was crescent-shaped and had a big smiley face, surrounded by twinkling white stars.
The other wall had a large sunshine with black sunglasses on it and depicted a beautiful, beach scene.
There was the sound of snuffling coming from the centre of the room as Charlie moved further in behind the wizard, through the low light he noticed around ten wooden cots, all filled with little babies.

Quiet, lullaby music played to soothe the babies in their land of slumber.
They were wrapped in blankets and sleeping soundly, except one at the end who had been woken by the noise of the men and the low lighting in the room.
The wizard comforted the child and rocked the cot.
Charlie continued to move about the room. There were five changing stands with cupboards underneath. Charlie looked at the wizard as if to ask if he could open the doors. The wizard smiled and nodded slowly.
Charlie opened the doors and found nappies, baby milk powder, baby wipes and further paraphernalia.
The baby that stirred was now fast asleep again and the wizard ushered Charlie to a door at the far end of the room. They walked through quietly. It was decorated magnificently, this time with lava lamps, fairy lights, coloured lights and large comfy sofas.
'A sensory room?'
'That's what you call it. Let's keep going.'
They walked on and through another door that took them back outside and into the cool night once more.
'What is this place?' Charlie said, more in awe than anything else.
'I understand you have questions, Charlie. Let's go to my abode and we can talk.'
Charlie followed the wizard across the courtyard to a pine lodge. The wizard opened the door and led Charlie inside.
'Have a seat. I'll make some tea.'
Charlie sat down on one of two comfy chairs that surrounded a wooden coffee table.
'Are you going to tell me what the hell is going on here?' Charlie said, trying to find some assertion,

remembering that despite the serenity, he was essentially a detective, investigating a crime.

'Charlie, that anger in you, it's not serving you. You don't need it…'

'I am just…'

'Confused. I understand.' the wizard said boiling an old, steel kettle on a hob. 'We built this community in the eighties. It was my friend and I who started it. We wanted to make something that was… different… you know… away from the world out there.'

'Like a commune, or a cult?'

The wizard laughed. 'Again, these are terms that are pejorative, to put labels on things that don't require them. There was a small group of us, who became sick and tired of certain aspects of modern life… and wanted something… different. Farming, aviary, living from the food and drink that we made, something more wholesome, if you will…'

'OK…'

The wizard poured from the kettle into two small silver cups.

'It grew through the nineties. There were a number of people who realised that a life with less distractions, away from technology and something more conscious, made them feel… better.'

'Right, OK, so how did we end up here, like thirty years later?'

'People have come and they have gone. But the core group stayed and then their children stayed and so we go. We continue on. It's a more moderate way of life. Pure.'

'I see… so who is looking after those kids now..?'

'Oh, there are around forty people living here now, fifty with the babies. We just take it in turns to monitor them overnight. Baby monitors are very much in use I must say!'

'Doesn't that go against your whole...*vibe?*'

The wizard laughed, 'what vibe?'

'Right. Well, as much as this seems idyllic and all that... you are kind've... sorry, but there is no other way to say this, *stealing babies?*'

'Not stealing, Charlie. You can't steal what doesn't belong to you.'

'But, these are people's kids! Mother's have gone through nine months of pregnancy and given birth and then... you take their sons and daughters?'

'The children are specially selected.'

'OK. Well would you care to elaborate?'

'The children are taken from parents who we know... are not good parents shall we say...'

'Yes, but who are you to decide who gets to keep their kids and who doesn't?'

'I decide nothing, Charlie. The parents do.'

'Wait? What?'

The wizard came to the table and placed the drinks down upon it, before sitting down in the spare chair.

'There is a database... parents of children who have history of class-A drug use, abuse to their children, violence... these are the babies we save.'

'*Save?*'

'From a life of pain, of sin, of being born into a corrupt world, traumatised and damaged by those who are supposed to love them.'

Charlie pondered what the wizard was saying. He couldn't quite believe what he was hearing, he needed time to digest all of this.

'Charlie, it's something that seems remarkable, something bad. But what we do is give these children

a chance. We love them, we care for them and then we set them free.'
'Set them free?' Charlie said, taking a drink from his cup.
'Yes, we give them the option when they are old enough to go back into that world or stay. It's up to them.'
'And what do they say?'
'It varies. Most stay, some take their chances. Some want to meet their mother's and try and help them... if they are still alive, that is. I appreciate it is a lot to take in, but there is a reason that you have found us here.'
'OK...' Charlie felt slightly woozy.
'And I need to tell you this, before you drift away...' the wizard continued.
The drink... what was in it...?
'I have been meeting with Stephen McCarthy, you know this. He is a great boy, a lovely boy, but his brother... is a danger, he's reckless. What they are doing at Highfield Industrial Facility is... unnatural...'
'Yeaah... like stealing kiddy-winks...'
Charlie was beginning to feel very hot, his vision was blurring and his eyes were rolling.
'I'm sorry, Charlie. You can't find out anymore about us. But don't worry, we will make sure you're safe. You need to stop Johnny. You need to get into that facility...'
Charlie tried to remain focused on the wizard's words, but the more he did, the more he found himself drifting into a cosy, calming sleep.

'It's that *bastard* I need to get next.' Johnny said,

raising his head and grabbing the bottle of vodka from the side.
'Yes, I think you are right, Johnny.'
'If it wasn't for him, keeping it secret, betraying me with my brother...'
'Yes, and keeping you out. In the dark, the brother who was left out, cut out, cut loose. Thanks to him.' Smith continued.
'He's supposed to love me unconditionally. But he fucked me off.'
'He did Johnny. He did.'
Johnny took another swig from the bottle.
'With his bloody robes and fucking hippie commune...'
'You need to find him soon, Johnny.'
'I have an idea where he is...'
'Yes, Johnny but you need to narrow it down, the marsh is big...'
'It's OK. I have got a lot of disciples working for me.'
'If it wasn't for him, your brother would be alive.'
Johnny took a deep breath and looked at Smith with dark, angry eyes. Smith steeled himself, worried he had gone too far.
'That's right. He's killed my brother. I'm going to get myself together, then I'm coming for him. You hear that, dad? I'm coming for you.'
Johnny staggered up from the table and left through the double doors.
Doctor Smith waited until the wiry frame of the last remaining McCarthy brother was out of view, before picking up his phone and dialling.
'Hi Will.'
'Hi Rob.'

'He's coming for you tonight. He'll bring the whole gang of delinquents. There will be twenty or so. Perhaps it's time to try out the new products…'
'Maybe, thanks for the heads up. And what about Stephen.'
'I am afraid its bad news, Will.'
There was a pause on the other end of the line, before the phone went dead.

27

There were pink clouds in the sky.

Charlie was lying on a grassy bank, looking at a beautiful vista underneath a large, perfect rainbow.

The sea lapped in the distance and from up where he was, it all seemed very beautiful.

Serene.

'I don't blame you, you know,' Tara said. She was sitting next to him, clutching her knees to her body, staring at the view. She turned to him and smiled. 'You know that, right?'

'How can you not? I mean, I came into your life... I was all bluster and attitude and...'

'... And I loved you. And you loved me. I knew what you were like. When I was pregnant with Ridley, and my hormones... I... left you, Charlie. I don't forgive myself for that.'

'Well, I guess I got you back,' Charlie said.

Tara laughed. Charlie laughed.

'Yep and now, I'm dead!' Tara laughed again. After a little while they stopped laughing and a tear formed in Charlie's eye.

'It's not funny. Really. I miss you so much and I don't know if I can...'

'Charlie, if you don't get yourself together... I'm going to...'

'Go on... what are you going to do?'

'I'll haunt you...'

'I'd like that...'

'I'll flirt with your dad up here...'

'He'd like that...'

'I'll... I'll... make it stop hurting.'

'It will never stop hurting...'

'You need to hurt a bit more big boy, then you need to get it together and bring up those beautiful children. If not for you, for them. And for me.'
Charlie was in floods of tears.
'I love you and I'm sorry.'
'I know you do, and I love you, and that will never change. I promise. But I got to go.'
'Please stay...'
'Nah, your dad wants to take me for a drink tonight!'
Charlie looked up at her smiling face.
'Just kidding. But seriously, I'm off.'
Tara kissed her husband for a final time, before disappearing into dust.

The sun streamed onto Charlie's face, waking him from a restful sleep.
He opened his eyes to the sight of his bedroom in Ashford. He felt happy, as if a weight had been lifted, as if there was hope, a purpose.
He got up and checked next door.
No Ridley.
Grabbing his phone, he noticed he had a number of messages and missed calls.
He immediately phoned his mother.
'How are you? How's everything?'
His mother yawned, 'Ridley's fine. Still in hospital. Stable.'
'Where are you?'
'I'm here. I tried to contact you, but couldn't get through.'
'Sorry, I… uh… was working, out in the marsh… no reception.'
'Well, I'm glad you are keeping busy, but you need to phone the doctor and make a decision about her little

tummy.'
'OK, I'm going to head up there.'
'Good thinking. Your friend Becky is there, she came and took over from me yesterday evening.'
'Is that so? Wow, OK. Listen, thanks mum. You have really been there for me recently.'
'Well, what did you expect? I am your mother and I love you. Keep me updated please.'
'Sure thing, mum. I love you too.'
Charlie got himself showered, changed and headed out to the hospital. He was overjoyed to see that his car was parked out the back in his parking space.
He got in and drove up to the hospital, wondering what it was the weird-robey dude had given him yesterday. I mean, he should be angry, but instead he felt an enormous sense of wellbeing, gratitude even.
He got his car back, he was dropped in bed and he felt fine, good even.
All he really remembered was glorious colours, awesome sparkles… it was like a fairytale… Charlie wondered, *did it even happen?*
As he pulled up to the hospital, he realised he hadn't even thought about drink or drugs. His cravings for alcohol had disappeared.
He felt energised.
Charlie made it onto the children's ward and found Becky dozing in a chair. He checked his watch, 9.23am. She must have been there all night.
'Hey, sleeping beauty,' he said in her ear and she awoke with a jolt.
'Oh geez, hey Charlie,' she said drowsily. Her tired, glassy eyes and blonde curls over her face, gave Charlie a brief glimpse into another side of his friend he hadn't seen. Her morning after face.

He liked it, she looked good.
She swung her long, blonde curls back into a ponytail and came to a little more.
'What's happening here? What has the doctor said?'
'Oh, not a lot. They wanted to see how she went overnight, and she did good. Then they need to discuss options for the exompa…'
'Exomphalos.'
'That's right. But they said they could only do that after another specialist had seen her this morning. As you always say, hurry up and wait!'
'Well yeah. My dad always said that. I just stole it from him. Let me see what the latest is.' Charlie said, moving towards Ridley's room.
'Cool, fancy a coffee?' Becky said, getting up.
'Sure thing. Black, like my soul. Here, take my card.' Charlie said, flinging his wallet in Becky's general direction.
Charlie continued into Ridley's room. There were four cots in total and thankfully, there were nametags above each, so the kids could be easily identified. Not that Charlie needed it, he could recognise Ridley's deep brown eyes and little nose anywhere.
He realized quickly that she wasn't in her cot. The other three babies were, but not Ridley. Charlie checked them again to ensure that she hadn't been placed in the wrong one, then quite rapidly began to panic.
Once again, the hospital seemed deserted. There were no nurses or doctors that he could see. Eventually, after running through the halls, he found what looked like a doctor, bustling through the corridor at pace.
'Excuse me, Ridley Stone. I'm looking for her. Do you know where she might be?'

'I'm sorry, sir I am late for...'
Charlie stood in front of the doctor and stopped him.
'Listen, my baby is missing. I need to find her.'
'Jesus, not another...'
'Wait, you know about the babies?'
'No, sorry. Let me see what I can find. Follow me.'
The doctor headed back to the pediatric area and picked up a bright pink clipboard.
'Hm...' he went to another room and then another before heading into Ridley's original room. She wasn't there and Charlie was beginning to get irate.
'Listen, I can't be having this. We have to find her. Now!'
The doctor looked puzzled. Then a nurse came in through the double doors behind them with a bundle in her hands.
'Ridley!' Charlie took his daughter from the woman.
'Bless her; she is such a good baby. Started crying though. Full nappy and we had run out on this ward!'
'Right...'
'I'll be on my way then sir...' the doctor said, nodding at Charlie.
'But wait one second. What did you say about missing babies?'
The doctor looked at the nurse who swiftly vacated the room.
'Uhm... I didn't...'
'Look, I'm a police officer... well... I'm not, but I used to be. You heard of Charlie Stone?' Charlie felt like a real idiot name-dropping *himself.*
'The uh Sunny Sands guy?'
'Yep. That's me. I'm a P.I. now, and I have been following this guy, who I think may have been taking babies from here.'

The doctor checked his surroundings, before leaning in to Charlie to whisper.
'Of course we know about it. We just... can't have it getting out. Luckily, of the seven babies stolen, *none* of the parents have gone public. I don't know whether they were paid off with NDA's or what, but not a single one has made a fuss! The last baby went yesterday afternoon.'
'Yes, I know I followed the guy. Unbelievably, the babies are safe.'
'What? Really?'
'Why are you so surprised?'
'Well...usually it's not a good ending in these... scenarios...'
'I know... but, listen... all I can say is that the babies are alive and well. And I know who is taking them and I am going to bring him to justice.'
'Spoken like a true policeman!'
'Not anymore, no thank you. Just a concerned citizen doing his bit. I don't think there will be any more missing babies for a while.'
'Well, good luck to you, Mr Stone. Thank you.'
The doctor reached out and squeezed Charlie's free shoulder. Charlie looked at his little baby's face and smiled.
'No-one is taking you anywhere, little beaut. Daddy's gonna keep you with him forever and ever. Well, maybe I leave you with Auntie Becky and Granny Wina a bit, so daddy can catch the bad guys. But after that, you're all mine!'
'Don't forget Maddie.' Becky said, watching him from the doorway.
He looked up and there she was, black knee-high boots, skintight jeans, a black top and a long brown

cardigan. She looked…
'I … uhm… sorry.'
'Don't say sorry! It was beautiful. You're getting good at this dad stuff.'
'Anyway, put her down and tell me about last night.'
'I think I'm going to keep hold of her, you know.' Charlie said.
Becky nodded as they headed to the seats.

Johnny McCarthy took a slug of vodka before addressing his troops.
The stench of strong marijuana smoke hung in the air of the courtyard. It was approaching 2pm and the weather was inclement to say the least. Thunder rumbled in the distance and dark clouds loomed ominously over the Downs behind them.
'Right guys, tonight you are going to follow Ron and me down to the Marsh. I have vague co-ordinates of where that hippie fuck will be. But his weird little commune is hidden. Well. He's been protected and hidden by powerful people for over forty years so this isn't going to be an easy job. But he's in there. All of you are coming with. We are bringing the dogs too. Torches, weapons the fucking lot all need to be brought. Sort it out amongst yourselves. We leave at 9pm.'
'Ere boss, how… uh… how are we going to find…'
'We are going to fucking look. And we aren't leaving until we find him. This old boy has messed everything up. If it weren't for him, my brother would still be alive.'
'Right…'
'Anyone else got a question?'
Johnny looked along the long line of black, nylon

jackets and woollen balaclavas.
No-one said a word.
'When we find them, the whole lot fucking goes. Spare none of them.'

Becky sat digesting the information that Charlie had just relayed, while he put his daughter back down in her cot.
Charlie returned and Becky appeared confused.
'So, let me get this straight. There's like a commune...'
'Yeah, but it's not bad or...'
'Whatever, Charlie. No matter how good the drugs were that they put in your drink, they are stealing kids and drugging members of the public...'
'Fair poin...'
'So, you are telling me there is a hidden commune somewhere in the marsh...'
'I think it's *under* the marsh, mainly...'
'Under the marsh, that's been there for decades, where they live like true flower children and liberate babies born into terrible lives?'
'That's the sum of it, yeah.'
'So, what's the connection with the McCarthy's?'
'Good question. I mean, this wizard-guy can't exactly walk into the William Harvey and start taking babies. Maybe they are the only guys who would do it...'
'But why would they get involved? What's in it for them?'
'He can't be paying them, surely?'
'No... did you see Johnny McCarthy at all?'
'Nope, just his brother. The uh... tubbier one.'
'Let's call him... the nicer one, eh?'
'In fact, Johnny has never been implicated in the baby

thing at all, right?'
'Not that I've seen...' Charlie confirmed.
'So maybe this is like... a personal thing... maybe Steve is doing it due to some kind of twisted kindness. Like he's trying to do something... good?'
'To counteract all of the gangster stuff...'
'Exactly. I mean, I have followed these guys for a couple of years now. They are brothers, bonded by blood. But they aren't like friends or close... it's like a business thing. Maybe this is Steve's little bit of goodness, a light through the gloom of the drugs and the trafficking and all the other shit they are tied up in...'
'It sounds feasible to me.'
'So, what are we going to do next?'
'Highfield Facility. All of the answers will be there. Confront Steve about the babies and find out what on earth the wizard was talking about. He said something dark was going on there.'
'Well, we do kinda know that, right? The testing? The immigrants?'
'Yeah, but I don't know. There may be more than that. Either way, there is only one way to find out.'
The doctor from yesterday poked his head around the door.
'Mr Stone, can you come through please?' he said.
'Listen, I'll go ahead to the facility. You stay here with Ridley.' Becky said hopefully, eager to get back to action.
'No way, Becky. Please... I can't... you know why I can't. Let's do this together. OK?'
'OK. But we need to get moving. Those babies might be safe, but it still isn't right... you know?'
Charlie wasn't sure. He could see the logic of the

wizard's actions. He saw the serenity of Notwell's, what the wizard had created and it made sense.
He shook himself back to reality.
How can it be OK? You can't steal babies, Charlie. Get a grip!
'I'll see you shortly,' Charlie said, turning the corner and into the doctor's office.
Becky sat and pondered this plethora of new information and tried to weigh it up with all of the research on the McCarthy's that she had previously done.
She felt a strong buzz of energy flow through her, like she wanted to get up, get going, get moving, like there was an impending sense of doom, like they were in the eye of the storm.
She checked the files on her phone, The McCarthy files, she had kept together and password protected.
Flicking through, she looked to find anything of note, to jog her memory.
Articles, case files, interview notes.
Then something caught her eye. An article she downloaded from a dubious website, filled with conspiracy theories, called Pandemonium.com.
Is a Third Reich weapons programme thriving in underground bunker in Kent?
Becky couldn't remember why she kept this article, so continued to skim read it.
Local reports suggest large-scale vehicles moving in and out of abandoned site...
Is toxic chemical weapon Tabun being investigated?
Biological warfare... Viral compounds...
It all seemed a little pie in the sky, but then she noticed why it was she had kept the article in the first place.

Government agent, William McCarthy, 27, has reportedly quit his post over the findings at the secret bunker in Kent. He was unavailable for comment…
Becky checked the date of the article… 1988… the dates fitted. *What if William McCarthy was the wizard? What if he was also…*
She closed her phone and ran to the exit of the hospital.

'Mr Stone, the good news is that little Ridley is doing well currently, she is stable and the issues that she had with her stomach appear to have abated…'
'Brilliant!'
'For now… however… her condition suggests that these problems may well come back and could cause digestion issues in the future…'
'Well… how bad are we talking…'
'It's difficult to say. Children with similar problems have been known to recover fully and some have had further complications.'
'Complications?'
'Yes.'
'Can you elaborate?'
'Well, if the problem persists and the organs are unable to correct themselves, it will mean that toxins will not go to the correct place and it can be… very serious.'
'Like, *serious?'*
'It can be fatal for some children.'
Charlie took a deep breath. 'So, what do you suggest?'
'It is a very tricky decision, Mr Stone. I mean there is a chance that the exomphalos will clear up on its own. Nevertheless, like I say, there is a chance it could

cause the issues that I have discussed.'
Charlie sat looking into the distance.
The thousand yard stare.
'Percentage- wise? What chance have we got if we don't operate?'
There was a bustling at the door, followed by a knock. Charlie turned around to see his mother standing in the doorway. He was relieved to see her.
'Mind if I come in?'
'No, please do, mum.'
She came and sat near Charlie on the second spare seat.
'What have I missed?' she said, curtly.
The doctor filled her in and without even pausing for thought, Charlie's mother had her response.
'If she is fine now, I suggest that we leave it. There is no need to put the little girl through an operation, she may not need.'
'But…'
'With operations on children so young there can be issues and complications, but conversely, she may be OK. She may be fine. She may live a life and never even know she had this problem.' She continued.
The doctor nodded sagely. Charlie held his head in his hands.
'What do you think, Charlie?' the doctor said slowly.
'Did you see Becky outside, ma?' Charlie asked.
'No, not outside. Why?'
'I just… listen, I need some time to think. I uh…'
Charlie did not know what to do. He wasn't qualified to make decisions such as this. His head dropped and he stared at the floor.
He felt the darkness setting in. The desire to drink rose in him, he clenched his fists and squeezed as

hard as he could until his knuckles went white, and veins popped in his hands.

'Charlie, may I make a suggestion? Let me take Ridley to my house. Give her a night or two there, in the quiet where she can rest and recuperate. You can come down when you wish, but it gives you time to think about what to do and time to strengthen her up and get her better. What do you say?'

Charlie looked at his mother through glassy, wet eyes.

'Thanks, mum.'

With that, there was a flurry of activity between the doctor and his mother as Charlie sat contemplative in his seat.

He couldn't cope with this. He just sat and imagined the sea, in and out, in and out, in and out. *Keep breathing, Charlie.*

Keep.

Breathing.

'Charlie? Charlie! Are you listening? I'm off. Are you coming? Or coming later? I don't mind either way.' his mother said.

Charlie couldn't respond.

'If you don't mind, Mrs Stone, I'll uhm…'

'It's McClinton actually…'

'Sorry, Mrs McClinton, if you don't mind, I might just keep him here for a moment. Make sure he's OK.' the doctor said.

'Fine. See you soon, Charlie.'

'OK…'

The doctor helped Charlie up and walked him to an empty room within the ward. He placed him on a spare bed and attached a blood pressure monitor.

'You know, Charlie, when we talked the other day, I

went home and googled you. You are a bonafide hero, you know that?'
'I'm not...'
'Listen, you have had some serious trauma in your life. The loss of loved ones, the closest people to you. And now this. I know you blame yourself for a lot of things, but none of it, not a single jot of it was your fault.'
'I led McCarthy to Tara...'
'Tara was with you because she loved you. He would have gone after anybody, anyone. Your kids, your mum. There was nothing you could do. Which is why once we have had a little check-up, you need to go and put that guy behind bars.'
'I killed Dave too...'
'No, Charlie. He loved you and wanted to help you. You're loved, Charlie. They loved you.'
'Hm.'
'Close your eyes now, Charlie.'
He did as he was told and drifted off into a relaxing dream.

Charlie looked out at the view, over the hills. The pink clouds were above him and the sea lapped gently on the shore to his right. The sun glistened upon the breaking waves.
'He can't do what he's doing, can he?' Charlie asked.
'No. I don't think so. But he's coming from a good place, it's just a bit misguided is all.' Tara said, leaning over to grab his hand.
'I am going to find it hard to bring him in.'
'It's a real moral conundrum, Charlie. And it's your choice, but imagine if it was... oh I can't even say

it...'
'If it was Ridley? Yeah, but he said he only takes from like,,, you know... drug addicts and criminals.'
'But who is he to decide? You can't play God like that. Life is like a box of chocolates and all that. You can't just have purple quality streets in a box.'
'God, why would you want that!?'
'That's why we worked. I liked the purple's, You ate everything else!'
They smiled and she pulled him closer for a hug.
'You can if you want, you know Charlie.'
'What?'
'You know what.' Tara smiled and stroked his face,
'I...'
'It's fine. I want you to be happy. Just don't forget about me, OK?'
'I couldn't if I tried!' he asserted through bleary eyes.
'Anyway, I am going for a drink with your dad, tonight in Luci's bar.'
'Funny.'
'No, I am. But trust me, he's not my type. But you are like him. You're like all of his good bits.'
'Thanks.'
'You're welcome. Now get back and find her. Quickly.'

Charlie awoke in the room.
The machine he was attached to bleeped lazily in the background.
There was no-one around, so he disconnected himself and snuck out. The doctor was nowhere to be seen. He made it out of the ward and into the main corridor that led to the exit.

His daughters were safe, but was his good friend Becky? He tried her phone. No answer. He tried it again, same result.
She must have headed to one place and one place only and it looked like Charlie was heading back to deepest, darkest Folkestone.

28

As Charlie drove the short stretch along the M20, his phone rang.
'Hey, Mad!'
'Hey, dad! How are you?'
'Yeah, not bad, hun. What about you? How's school?'
'School has been fine, dad. We are learning about Tudor England at the moment in English, which is kinda cool.'
'Oh, nice one! When do you reckon we can meet up next?'
There was a pause.
'Not sure you know, because of mum. But I am going to ask her if I can visit soon, maybe on the weekend?'
'That would be great, Mad. You know you are always welcome.'
'Listen, dad. I got this uh… you know, feeling and I just wanted to know whether Ridley was OK?'
'Wait, did Becky speak to you?'
'No. I text her to say hi, but apart from that, no.'
'So how do you know?'
'Dad, we talked about this!'
'Sorry! Yes, yes we did. She is… I mean, she was poorly.' Charlie wondered about how much he should tell his twelve-year-old daughter, but then realised that in fact, she seemed to know more about stuff than he did. 'Remember she was born with that little problem?'
'Yeah, with her tummy?'
'That's right. There was a little issue with that and we had to see a doctor…'

'In the hospital?'
'That's right. But she is out of the hospital and now she is with Granny Wina, being looked after at her house.'
'She's not at our house?'
Charlie smiled at the word 'our.'
'Not at the moment, it's quieter and more chilled down there.'
'Yeah, makes sense. Plus, you have got to work, I guess?'
'That I have.'
'Well, I think Ridley is going to be OK. I woke up last night and was really worried. But as the day has gone on, I'm feeling brighter, happier. I think she will be OK. I think just… give her time and she will get better on her own.'
'You think?'
'Yep.'
'OK, well that's good, Mad.'
'So Dad, I want to come down soon. Be ready for me!'
'Always, sweetheart.'
'Love you.'
'Love you too.'
Charlie turned off the motorway for Folkestone and the time was coming up to 6.30pm.
The light was fading fast.
He pulled up on Dover Road and decided to walk along to the Industrial facility where he believed Becky to be.
He couldn't see her car anywhere, but he pressed on regardless, moving towards his target. *How would she get in*? He wondered.
She would have crept in the way they did last time,

barging through the front door was not an option.
Charlie double-backed, up Dover Road and along to the toothpaste factory, making sure not to be seen as he crept through the area. He followed the exact same path as they did last time.
Past the Life Church on the right and behind the large pallets that were stored outside the metal warehouse to his left. As a large truck pulled out of the facility, it gave Charlie enough cover to be able to squeeze past the security guard in the booth and into the belly of the beast.
He skipped over the old outhouses and derelict buildings and when he arrived at the manhole cover, he noticed it was loose. This pleased him, as it was the confirmation he needed that he was hopefully on the same path as Becky.
Down and along, quietly opening the second cover in the courtyard... This time there was lots of movement to his left. There were people, dogs, bright lights, motorcycles, cars, so Charlie put the cover back down and decided to find another entrance.
He kept moving, using his light from his phone as a torch. About twenty yards further along, he found another cover and began to unscrew it. This time it was in a more secluded part of the facility, behind the old, dilapidated house that they surveyed from last time.
It was also the place where Becky was taken.
Charlie steeled himself and pulled himself out of the ground, he got to his feet and then knelt down. It was quiet where he was, but he could hear the commotion in the centre of the courtyard.
He moved slowly and quietly towards the old building. He crept inside and could feel the presence

of another body in the vicinity. He climbed through the window and then up onto the roof, where he was greeted by the blonde, curly hair and the big broad smile of his friend.
'Fancy seeing you here,' he said.
'What are the odds?'
'It does seem strange that you would come back to the exact place where you were captured and imprisoned last time…'
'Oh, fear not. A wise man once told me lightning never strikes twice. Oh wait? It wasn't a wise man, it was you!' Becky joked.
'All banter aside, what in the holy hell do you think is going on here?'
'They are preparing for something. Preparing to move out. Looks like all of them. Weapons. Dogs. Vehicles. The lot.'
'I see. That will leave the facility empty, so we can look around.'
'Charlie, you need to see something.' Becky got out her phone and showed Charlie the article that she saw earlier.
'When I first saw it, I didn't take it that seriously as you know… it just seemed a little far-fetched, but…'
'Hey, Bex? You ever try to read while someone's talking at you?' Charlie smiled.
'Sorry! Sorry.'
Becky hushed and Charlie read the article.
'Shit. This makes sense now. The wizard, he is the McCarthys' dad. That's why the bigger one…'
'The *nicer* one…'
'Yeah, he is working for his dad! Getting the babies out.'
'But the other one, Johnny. He has nothing to do with

it. He runs this place. So maybe, dad has got a favourite son and this is why it looks like these guys are going to battle?' Becky mused.
'You think so?'
'I haven't seen Steve once and I have been here for over an hour. The other one keeps coming out, barking orders, but Steve is nowhere to be seen. Perhaps he is with the wizard now…'
'That would make sense.'
'And these guys are coming for them…'
'Maybe. But they are going to have a job finding them.' Charlie added.
'I mean… not being funny Charlie, but you found them…' Becky smiled. 'First time looking, but you know, I'm sure it was *very hard.*'
'It was more luck than judgment, that's for sure.'
'Here.'
Becky passed Charlie a pair of binoculars and he watched as three young lads revved up their motorbikes and made their way to the metal gate.
'Right, let's get moving. No point in waiting around.'
Charlie checked his watch, 7.30pm.
He watched through the binoculars as Johnny McCarthy and his henchman, Ron, got into a car and headed out. Two boys opened the gate then hopped on their bikes and followed.
Then there was a large Luton van, followed by another four motorcycles. The last person out, stopped and locked the large gate behind them before speeding off to catch the rest of the group.
'Now's our chance to have a proper look around, it's deserted.' Becky said.
They got up from their position and made their way back down to the floor and into the facility with the

fluorescent lights. Charlie remembered the Doctor from last time, so ushered Becky to creep quietly and slowly into the building.
They went in and heard the buzzing of machines, alongside a mechanical hum, coming from the farthest lab. Charlie stayed low and moved stealthily towards it, checking the rooms as he went.
Deserted.
He turned the corner quickly into the final room and noticed a large silver table in the centre of it. Upon it, lay the body of Steve McCarthy.
'He's dead! He's been beaten up badly too,' Charlie said. 'He's been done by his own gang, his own boys, but why?'
'Betrayal, Charlie. And now his brother is going to finish the job by killing his father.' Becky responded.
'But there's no one there to protect them? What about the babies?'
'I don't know…' Becky said.
'I… we have to get down there and try and warn them, try and protect them.'
'But, Charlie, they are already on their way!'
'Yes, but I know a secret entrance…'
'Charlie, it's too dangerous… '
'Come on Becky, I'm not leaving those babies at the mercy of Johnny McCarthy and his mob of hoodlums. No way.'
Becky pondered, 'but this is our chance of finding out what is *really* going on here.'
There was silence between the pair. A moment of calm, of wondering, before the sound of a metal door in the distance clanked open.
'Hide, get low.' Charlie said.
Becky hid behind a desk and Charlie behind the

door.
A moment later, Doctor Robert Smith came bustling into the room and towards the body of Steve McCarthy.
After a few moments, the doctor grabbed his phone, took off his white jacket and replaced it with a black leather one. He then exited the room, down the corridor and out of the facility.
'Dinner break?'
'Who knows, but let's be quick in case he comes back.'
Becky rifled through his pockets to find his keys.
'Listen, Becky. I can't leave those kids to that madman.'
'OK, so what are you going to do?' How are you going to stop that mob? What's our plan, Charlie? If we go with them, we will go down with them.' Becky spluttered, almost guilty at her own words.
'I can't leave them. But, I don't want to leave you.'
'Stay here with me and we will find out what's going on. These keys, this keycard… it looks far too sophisticated for this to be some backwater operation. Charlie, I don't want you to go. You can't risk it.'
Charlie paused and took a moment to think.
'You are right. It's too risky. Let's focus on what's happening here.'
'I know it's not ideal at all, Charlie but your kids need you. I need you. Alive and around, OK?' Becky said, moving towards him and holding his hands.
'OK… I get it.'
'Thank you. Now follow me.'
Becky sneaked with Doctor Smith's key card down the hall, she remembered from the article it said something about a secret door.

'Char, what did it say in that article about a... Charlie? *Charlie?*'
Becky turned around but she was on her own.
Charlie Stone was nowhere to be seen.
'Jesus, Charlie!'
It was no use, he was long gone. Becky had a decision to make. Carry on with her search or follow Charlie Stone.
She settled on both. First, to investigate this facility.
She walked along the corridor, before moving through each cell, using Robert Smith's keycard to let herself in.
She came to the final one and noticed something different about it. It was smaller and impractical due to its size.
She noticed a vent on the ceiling, which could lead somewhere, but then when she moved towards the back wall she noticed that there was a large door-shaped ridge, that was barely noticeable, unless of course, you were looking for something just like this.
She found a keyhole covered with a protector and tried a number of keys in the lock, none of which worked.
Eventually, after quite some effort, she struck gold and the key turned.
There was the sound of metal upon metal, and Becky was able to push the large heavy door open, before heading down the dark steps and into the unknown.

The car roared along the A2070 into the lowly wasteland of the Romney Marsh. The road was unusually quiet. He wondered what it must have been like with the McCarthy mob eating up the tarmac, some moments before.

Charlie dialled in a number and waited.
'Charlie! Long time no speak!'
'Hey Jacko, listen I need some support… some back up…'
'What's going on?'
'Johnny McCarthy is on the rampage.'
'Oh, Jesus. You haven't upset him?'
'Not me. Well, yes me, but more importantly, his father…'
There was a pause.
'Charlie, his father disappeared years and years ago, after all that underground bunker malarkey…'
'I know, listen, there is lots I have to fill you in on mate, but trust me, we have a problem and lots of people are in serious danger. Lots of kids. Babies.'
'Jesus…'
'I need you to find Notwells Farm, Old Romney. The gang are there…'
'Charlie, I'm losing you… '
Jacko!'
The phone line went dead and Charlie realised that he had no reception on his phone. The joys of being on the marsh.
He reached the turning that led to the farm and immediately dimmed his lights on the car to avoid any form of detection.
'Sheesh!' Charlie was surprised how dark it was when the lights were off. It was literally pitch black as he drove towards the factory at snail's pace.
To his left, he could see a flurry of torchlight and the sound of shouting, orders being given… dogs barking…
He pressed on, along the straight road, holding the steering wheel as tight and as precisely as he possibly

could. After a few moments, he realised that this was sheer madness, as he could see nothing in the darkness. If he hit a tree or curbed it and got a flat, then he would be more likely to be found, not to mention if he needed to make a quick getaway later.

He stopped his vehicle in the middle of the road, and continued on foot towards the farm. To his left, the sound of dogs growling and barking closed in, nearer to him. Charlie used the light from his phone screen, which dimly lit a path ahead.

He took a detour into the woodland in an attempt to provide cover for himself. He knew that the outside wall of Notwells should be up ahead.

He was coming in from a different angle than before, so it was going to be a challenge, as he knew the route from last time, the landmarks, the trees he saw, but this time he would have to wing it.

'Ere the dog's got a scent!' came a shout from behind him.

Charlie was certain that the pack was getting nearer. He picked up his pace and clambered through the undergrowth and trees. He stumbled and lost his footing, landing face-first in a patch of stinging nettles. He picked himself up and continued on his path, scampering forward, always forward, but it was slow progress in the dark of the wood.

A beast growled. It was so near that he froze. He looked in the darkness and saw its beady eyes through the murk. The animal leapt and clamped its jaws around the back of Charlie's leg. He wanted to scream but suppressed the urge. He turned and pulled the dog from him, flinging it through the darkness.

It's beady, glassy eyes were all he could see in the night, until the beast bared it's teeth and growled once more, sprinting and launching himself at Charlie for a second time.

Charlie didn't have time to mess around. The rottweiler was large, powerful and trained to kill. In addition, the under-19's that were following will be here any minute.

As Charlie tussled with the animal he remembered something that his grandfather taught him many years ago. He reached and grabbed its two front legs and pulled them directly to ninety-degree angles. The beast yelped in agony as its front legs were broken and its torso ripped open.

Gravity pulled it to the ground and the dog lay whimpering, waiting for death.

Charlie swallowed, realising this was not his finest hour, but needs must. He could hear the men drawing nearer, so he continued to run towards the farm. As he got nearer to the side wall, he sped up, forgetting about the five foot drop that awaited him.

Over he tumbled and down, down to the hard ground beneath him. He rolled and took a large amount of the fall on the upper part of his right arm. Pain shot through his torso and again he gritted his teeth, while taking a moment to internalise rather than externalise his agony.

He listened and could still hear commotion above him. He stayed still and quiet, trying to ascertain where his enemies were.

'Charlie…' a gravelly voice whispered in the darkness.

He looked towards the wooden door to see the wizard ushering him into the sanctuary of their hidden home.

Charlie got to his feet and moved apace into the tunnel, before the door slammed behind them.

'How did you know I was there?'

'We have some technology…' the wizard spoke calmly.

'I could see that someone, something was moving towards us. I could also see that after all this time, finally he is coming.' the wizard said prophetically.

'Johnny? Your son?'

The wizard looked at Charlie before speeding up the tunnel towards the other door.

'We need to get the children out before he gets here. He has his gang of hoodlums with him… dogs, weapons… the lot.'

'Come inside,' the wizard said, opening the front door.

'Are you not worried?'

'Worried? About seeing my son?'

'Yes, but he has come for vengeance… he thinks… he blames you for having to kill his brother!'

Charlie nodded and the wizard hung his head.

'Then let him come to try and take what he wants.'

'He wants *you. Dead.*' Charlie said, trying to explain the urgency of the situation.

The wizard just smiled.

'What have I told you, Charlie? *Relax.*'

29

Becky slowly descended the metal staircase into the darkness below.
She could hear the sound of something mechanical and people working, but she couldn't see her hand in front of her face.
She stopped and got her phone from her pocket and was relieved to have one tiny little bar of reception, so she texted Charlie:
Final cell, back wall, door unlocked. I am going in.

She put the phone away, continued down the metal steps, and began to notice a small blinking light ahead of her in the distance. She focused on it and realised that it led down to another security door.
She held Doctor Smith's keycard against the blinking red light until the blinking stopped and the large metal door slid open.
Becky found herself at the top of another large stairwell that looked down upon an even larger factory floor. There were a number of people below, so Becky immediately ducked down to hide from view. She waited a moment and then peeked down the metal stairs and onto the factory floor.

There were armed security guards, watching approximately thirty men work on what looked like a large silver machine in the centre of the room.
It must have been around twenty metres in width and ten in height, and looked like something that she had never seen before. It was orb-shaped, completely smooth, and in many respects, other worldly.
Becky double backed on herself and re-opened the security door behind her. She placed Doctor Robert

Smith's keycard on the floor outside. If she needed saving, if Charlie came back for her, he would need it to get in.
Becky began to descend the stairwell once more as quietly as she could. There were large metal railings that provided cover for her as she moved down, but she was vulnerable and unarmed in a hostile and top secret environment.
As she got nearer, in between the sounds of metalwork and ongoing movement, she could hear the sound of whimpering, of the worker's weeping. She noticed that a number of them were totally emaciated, if one of them stopped working for a brief moment, the guards barked at them, if they stopped again they were beaten.
One man fell to the floor through what appeared to be sheer fatigue.
'Get up, *now!*' came the order from one of the armed guards.
But he couldn't, his eyes had closed. The guard pulled him to the centre of the room, then he grabbed his gun and with the butt of it, proceeded to smash the man's skull until the floor was covered in crimson and his body was limp.
'You two, clean this up! Take him to the dump!'
Two men scurried towards the dead body, their sharp ribs seemed to be poking through their brown flesh, and took the body by the arms and legs.
That would explain the chimney, Becky thought. *They are burning the bodies.*
She took a deep breath and tried to prevent tears falling from her eyes.
She looked down to find somewhere she could hide on the floor of the facility.

There was a door ajar at one end, but she couldn't be sure if somebody was in the room or not. Two guards came together and started talking in loud voices.

As they did Becky scampered down and hid behind a tall metal shelving unit in the corner of the factory floor.

She made it without being seen, however, one of the immigrants, a younger man who seemed fitter, fleshier than a lot of the others came across to the shelves, to pick up a tool.

Becky tried to remain still, cowering behind a large tool box in the corner, but it was futile. Their eyes met and the man's eyes widened in surprise. Becky put her finger to her lips and hoped the man would stay silent.

He said nothing, picked up the tool that he required and went back to the large, silver orb.

Becky breather a large sigh of relief and took a moment to look up at the behemoth in front of her.

There was a strange humming sound, something ethereal, something strange, like the machine was alive.

Becky corrected herself, how can it be alive? It's a bloody machine!

At least it appeared to be a machine, but unlike anything she had seen before.

She tried to see what it was that the men were doing, but again it was alien to her. They were using specific tools that were unlike any she had seen in her lifetime… cylinders that glowed with bright white light. The men kept putting them into the orb and then taking them out, replacing them with new ones and putting the old ones onto a rack.

'Someone's in here! Guards! Guards!' came a voice

from above her, upon the stairwell.
The worker from earlier slowly came back to where Becky was, and pretended to be getting something else from the shelving unit. The man looked her in the eyes
'Second door on the right-hand wall, see?' he whispered, nodding his head towards the wall on Becky's left and a door that had a green fire exit sign above it, Becky nodded.
'Help these people.'
'I will.' she returned.
The man turned and moved back towards the orb.
'Look, they must be in here! My card was left outside! We have to find them, no-one can know about this operation!'
'AAAAAHHH!' Came the cry from the centre of the room as the man who approached Becky, launched himself at another worker. He rolled on top of him, causing a great commotion, and more importantly, providing a distraction which saw the guards sprint towards them to separate the men.
The doctor watched on and Becky realised that this was her chance to make a run for the room. She went low and fast and as she got there, made sure she shut the door silently behind her.
Inside, was an office, but most pertinently there was a desk with a small wooden truncheon on it, presumably one of the guard's. Becky grabbed it and turned around before two loud gunshots echoed through the building followed by silence.
Becky was angry now, but had to retain her focus. She peeked out the top of the window and saw the ruckus. Within minutes, the workers were back to working or staring aghast. The two guards had

separated and the man in the white coat, Doctor Robert Smith, was gesticulating wildly.
She noticed a guard heading to this side of the room, so she ducked down. He went to the third door just beyond the office she was in now. He opened it and went in, before coming out and slamming the door behind him.
Becky hid under the desk to maintain cover, just in case he looked in through the window before entering. She heard the door creak open and watched, as the black boots of the guard came toward her position. She had no option, so she swung hard and fast at the guard's kneecaps, which saw him crumple to the ground.
She moved from under the desk and into the open and she saw the angry black eyes as his hand reached towards her face. Before he made contact, Becky hit him twice, hard, on the back of the head with the truncheon, causing him to crumple further into a ball on the floor.
Becky moved past his body and looked out of the window of the door. Smith was not in view and the second guard was searching with his gun cocked and loaded.
The door was slightly ajar so Becky shut it and moved the body of the unconscious guard into the corner of the room, facing the wall. She went back to the door and banged on it twice, before heading back into a cover position.
'Keiran? Are you OK? What the hell…' the guard opened the door and as he did Becky launched herself at him and attacked him with the truncheon. This time, however, he was wise to it and cracked her hard on the jaw with the rifle butt. The guard followed up

with a swift right boot to Becky's face, as she fell to the floor.
There was a crunch of bone and gristle as the guard pulled her by the hair and out into the main hall.
'Found her!' he shouted.
'*Her? Really?*' Smith said, just before Becky faded from consciousness.

Charlie followed the wizard to a small office that nestled just behind the wooden lodge.
Inside the office, there were security cameras and some incredibly high tech computer equipment.
'Jeez, I... uh,' Charlie started before sitting down in an office chair beside the wizard.
'You are surprised at all of this?'
'Yeah, I am...'
'Appearances can be deceptive, Charlie,' the wizard said zooming in on the baying mob that were currently scouring the inside of the abandoned farm around thirty metres above their current location.
'Shit, they are right on top of us. We need to get everyone out. If you create a distraction, I can get them out the back...'
'Relax, Charlie...'
'Relax? *Relax?* That's all you seem to say! These people are coming to kill you! We need to do something! I have called for backup, with any luck...'
'Police? They won't come out here...'
'I know the guy. He's a friend of mine...'
'Even so.'
'Well, what are we going to do?'
'Wait and watch.'
Charlie watched the screen, there were dogs and

around ten of McCarthy's boys, looking through the old equipment and abandoned machinery of the farm.
The wizard pressed a button on his complex bit of kit and immediately, the song 'Always on my Mind' by Elvis began playing through a speaker that was placed at the furthest point from the only exit of the abandoned farm.
The mob looked confused and bewildered, slowly moving towards the speakers where the music was coming from.
There was shouting, hollering, excitement even at the thought that their search for the old man may well have been over.
Maybe I didn't love you…
After the last of the lads on motorbikes entered the old farm, McCarthy's car drove up and onto the tarmac behind them.
Maybe I didn't hold you…
'What is this whack music, fam?'
'Fuck knows, innit? This place is bear weird…'
The driver's side door of Johnny's car opened, but then after a few moments, shut again with no-one getting out.
'Come on, son. Don't be shy.' the wizard said, his finger stroking a large black button on the console in front of him.
The kids became restless as the chorus kicked in and the music blared from the speaker. Two of them began to inspect it, attempting to remove it from the strong, metal pole that fixed it to the ground.
'What are you doing?' Charlie asked.
'Wait for it…'
'Do you want them to find you?'
The wizard looked at Charlie and smiled, 'they

won't.'
As the crowd within the farm became restless, they all started to move towards the speaker.
'Here we go…' the wizard said, as he pressed the black button down fully.
As he did, a clear and colourless gas pumped powerfully from an opening under the speaker, that the under-19's failed to notice. Clouds wafted into the mob's face and began to spread further afield.
'What the hell is that?' Charlie asked.
'Tabun…'
'*Tabun?* The nerve agent? Turn it off!' Charlie screamed.
'Too late…'
Like a horror movie from his worst nightmares, the kids in balaclavas began to scream and wretch, arms flailing, grabbing one another, grabbing their throats before falling to the ground, writhing in turmoil.
Charlie reached over and pressed the black button repeatedly to no avail.
'Turn it off!'
It was no use, the nerve agent had passed through the systems of practically all of McCarthy's men.
Charlie watched the screen as the teenagers fell to the floor, while McCarthy's car reversed and headed out of the farm at speed. One of the lads on a motorbike attempted to drive away, but just the small amount of gas he had inhaled was enough to send him ploughing into the large, wooden wall and then flailing onto the ground.
After sixty more seconds, the farm was still again. Littered with dead bodies, as Elvis sang the final notes of his classic hit.

Becky awoke to the sound of a computer buzzing and whirring behind her.
She opened her eyes and saw the guard in the main facility, watching his subjects who were furiously working on the large orb, anxious not to meet the same fate as their co-workers earlier.
As Becky came to, she noticed for the first time that the orb wasn't sitting on anything, it was literally hovering in mid-air.
She felt a mixture of blood and phlegm hit the back of her throat from her nose and coughed violently forward, half into the gaffer tape that was around her mouth and half out of her nose.
'You are awake.' the doctor said, moving towards her, ripping the tape from her mouth.
'Who the hell are you and why are you here?' he said bluntly.
'I'm an investigator…'
'Bloody typical. The minute those hoodlums leave the site, we get our first reporter in years…decades even!'
'I'm not a reporter.'
'Well, who do you work for then?' Smith raised his voice, as the guard's attention was caught and he began to walk slowly towards the small office.
'I don't work for anyone. I work for myself.'
'Bullshit!' The doctor had a Taser in his hand and used it on Becky, causing her to convulse aggressively in her chair. Her hands, which were taped and tied, smashed violently against the metal base where she was sitting. She screamed.
The guard was at the door now smiling as he watched the young, blonde girl, splattered in her own blood, writhing in the chair.

The doctor looked at the guard with disdain.
'I need to know where she comes from. How she knew we were here!' he shouted, before returning to his computer.
The guard smiled and placed the barrel of his rifle on Becky's face, the cold tip shocked her a little and she recoiled. The guard smiled at her, as he ran the rifle down her body, across her breasts and stomach and down into her abdomen, pushing against her pubic bone.
She winced, the air forced from her body. Tears formed in her eyes.
'Tell him what he needs to know…' the guard said slowly.
'There's nothing to tell… I saw a newspaper article… I…'
The doctor shook his head disbelieving, indicating for the guard to continue his dirty work.
The guard wore black leather gloves and thrust his hand out and clasped Becky's breast. His face was contorted with anger as he squeezed and squeezed with all his might twisting and turning…
As tears poured down Becky's face, she hadn't realised that the workers had taken an interest in what was happening to her, in the small room just to the side of the factory floor.
A handful of the younger, fitter men had moved towards the room, and before the doctor could bark his futile orders, they had rushed the solitary guard, disarmed him and were in the process of subduing him.
'Get back to work, scum! Do as I tell you! More men will be here any minute! *With dogs!* Get back to work! Or you will regret it!' he uttered.

The workers untied Becky and one man handed her a cloth for her bleeding nose.
She walked towards the doctor, who was now cowering in a corner, away from the men and struck him with a hard fist across the jaw.
He yelped in pain, before Becky cracked him again this time clean on the nose. As claret ran from his nostrils, the doctor became incensed.
'This bloody bitch! Who do you think you are? You don't understand!' he spluttered.
Becky, with the help of two workers, placed Doctor Smith in a seat and tied him to it.
'Thankyou for saving me. Thank you' Becky said somewhat overwhelmed, endorphins and adrenaline coursing through her body.
'No, thank you.' one of the men said solemnly.
'Go… go now… before they come back.' Becky said.
'What about you?'
'I want a word with the doctor here.'
'But what about the rest of them? They will be coming.'
'It's OK, I have someone coming too.' Becky smiled.

30

Charlie was left aghast.
'What… but why..?'
'Charlie, you know why.'
'But… you killed them, these kids…'
'They were evil people.'
'And you are not?'
The wizard laughed before getting up and heading back to the lodge. Charlie followed.
'Hey, we need to discuss this! I came to help you and not only are you stealing babies from the hospital, you have just murdered a group of teenagers!'
'Charlie. This is not what you think it is.' the wizard was rushing around, collecting items, packing things away.
'Well, explain it to me!'
'It's too late for that. Are you going to arrest me? I have broken the law, like you said.'
Charlie weighed up the situation. *The wizard was a murderer, that's for sure... but he was protecting the children. He has taken people, babies, who do not belong to him, but is he saving them from a fate that is worse?*
'You know that what I am doing here is pure and good, Charlie…'
'What? Like gassing people with nerve agent?'
'I am protecting what we have! Protecting what has been built! Something honest and good… a place that is better than the world out there. Drugs, depression, darkness… our place is beyond that, a slice of the future by going back to the past. Don't tell me, Charlie, that you think I'm wrong. Don't tell me that I'm the one in the wrong!'

Charlie was frozen, stuck in time between ideology and responsibility.
'Time is ticking, Charlie. So, what's it going to be?'

Becky pushed Smith back into the chair.
He was wriggling and writhing, raging that this young female upstart had overcome him.
Becky watched the last of the migrant workers escape up the stairs. They left one of the sub-machine guns with Becky, and took one with them as they escaped into the Folkestone night.
Ripping the tape from the doctor's mouth sharply, Becky sat down and waited for him to cease cursing.
'I would like you to tell me what is going on here, and explain to me, what on earth *that* is..' Becky said, pointing at the large orb that no longer hovered but was now sitting silently on the factory floor.
'You wouldn't understand the work that we are doing here!'
'Try me!'
The doctor harrumphed. 'Well, since you seem to have the upper hand, I suppose I have no option but to divulge… in layman's terms the vessel that you see behind you, is a UAP which crash landed on the marsh decades ago.'
'A UAP? Like a spacecraft?'
'Something like that.'
'Woah…' Becky turned to take in the large, silver craft, its slick and impressive curves, its unique shape and design.
'Yes, it is remarkable. It has helped us shape many facets of our modern life…'
'So, you have used alien technology?'
'Jeez, you really know nothing do you? We have

attempted to use the craft and reverse engineer its technology, which in turn has led to unprecedented advances in our own developments. We believe that although this vessel appears to be a metallic craft, that it is also, and I appreciate this sounds far-fetched to the average person, in some respects, *a living organism.'*

'That's what the migrants were doing? Keeping it... *alive?*'

'Correct.'

'That's why it was making noise and hovering?'

'Genius!'

'And they were feeding it those cylinders...'

'Bingo. Well done. Except now of course, because you have let all of them escape, this rather top secret government project is jeopardised, and the best chance we have ever had as a human race to make contact with other worlds is gone.'

'Why migrants?'

'Why the hell not, eh? It's the perfect crime. They come in, we use them, run them into the ground and kick them out. They say anything to anyone, the McCarthy boys resolve it. No-one believes them anyway. Kick up a fuss, engage the EDL. Undermine their limited existence. Use social media... Facepack, Twatter... whatever you lot call it and get the general public to despise them. Simple. It's the perfect crime.'

'Where did it come from? This... spaceship?'

'It's not a spaceship like from a different planet. This isn't the movies, Miss. But thankyou, for finally asking a half decent question! Well, it came, we believe, from... wait for it... out of the sea. As it travelled over the marsh, something caused the craft to malfunction and then it crash-landed, just outside of Old Romney. Trust me, we were as surprised as you are, that these... *extra-terrestrials...* were visiting this part of the world. We thought alien sightings were confined to more exotic places, but lo and behold, here we are.'

Becky looked again at the craft, its magnificence... its glory. The wiry frame of Johnny McCarthy moving towards her, cut the moment of awe and wonderment short. She raised her gun and aimed it at him.

'Now, now pussycat...'

'Where's Charlie?'

'Your guess is as good as mine, sweetheart. I haven't touched him, I promise.'

'Where the fuck is the wizard?' Johnny aimed at the doctor.

'Should be where we said. You didn't find him?'

'Erm, no. What did happen though, is my men got gassed. All of them, even Ron. Some toxic nerve agent it would seem. Whilst listening to fucking *Elvis* of all things.'

'Oh no, he used the tabun...' the doctor asked.

'The what? He used the... you knew that he had some deadly gas, but... you let us head down there anyway?' Johnny said, becoming more perplexed.

'Johnny McCarthy! This is bigger than you and your little mob of...of... *wankers!* You, my little hoodlum friend, were nothing and nobody until you met...'

Becky watched as the bullet hit the doctor's skull and a large patch of blood washed over the pastel green wall behind them. Becky then turned to see Johnny McCarthy, teeth clenched, pistol in his hand.

She aimed her gun to Johnny's torso, while he

pointed his towards her.
'Well now we have a little bit of a predicament, don't we?' Johnny said. 'I don't want any trouble with you, but I do want to know where my father is…'
'Your father. Will McCarthy. Willy the wizard?'
'Something like that. The old goat. He ruined everything for my brother and me. He plundered us into this life. Now I am serious, I have no need to hurt you. I could have killed you before when you trespassed here… remember? I could have got my boys to do a right number on a pretty little thing like you. But I didn't. I showed you mercy. '
'Make no mistake Johnny, this machine gun will cut through you before you even get the chance to pull your little trigger,' Becky said confidently.
'Oh, bless. Thing is sweetheart, you don't even know how to use it. My guess is that the safety is still on.'
'Shall we find out?' Becky said. Their eyes met and for the first time in her life, Becky felt in full flow.
She was adrenalised, excited, engaged.
She was where she wanted to be.
All of a sudden there was an almighty crash and the door to the facility was busted open. Down came Charlie Stone at full pelt. As Becky watched her unarmed, fairly useless knight in shining armour, Johnny took the opportunity to grab hold of Becky from behind, placing one arm around her neck and his gun to her head.
'Drop the gun, now. *Drop it.*'
Reticently, Becky did as she was told. The machine gun fell to the floor and Johnny kicked it away out of their reach.
'Johnny, there's no need to be hasty pal, no more blood needs to be spilled today,' Charlie said.

'And no more will, Charlie. I just want to know where he is. In fact, Charlie I want to know how to get in to find him.'
'Johnny, I can tell you that. But just let her go.'
'No, Charlie!' Becky screamed.
'Listen, let her go, Johnny. And I'll give him to you. I promise.'
'A promise, eh? I've had a few of those. They never seem to work out for me. Anyway, I ain't stupid. Tell me, and I'll let her go.'
'Notwells farm… if you follow the perimeter through the woods around to the right, you will come to a big drop…'
'Charlie, you don't have to do this.' Becky remonstrated.
'... It's about five feet down and under the bushes and the undergrowth, there is a wooden door that leads to a tunnel. Through that tunnel, you are into his compound. That's it. Now let her go.'
Johnny pondered his options.
'The thing is Charlie, what if you are lying? Or he's already in custody? Or you let him go?'
'I promise you. I left him there. I could have apprehended him, I didn't.'
'You didn't, eh? And why's that? Show an old man some mercy? Give him kudos for killing my men? Killing my brother?'
'No, for what it's worth, I was disgusted by that little… show of might… but… what can I say, Johnny. It's complicated.'
'Complicated?'
'I used to think everything was black and white, Johnny. You killed my wife, Johnny. The woman I loved. I want you dead more than anything else in the

world. But I also want to make sure the things I love that are left… are safe. I haven't done a good enough job at keeping people safe.'

'How very fucking sweet. The thing is, Charlie, I'm not sure I believe you, see? I think you might be lying. So I'm taking this one with me.'

Johnny began to back away up the stairs, Becky in a chokehold, Charlie edging towards the machine gun lying on the floor. Johnny shot his gun towards Charlie and hit the orb.

'I like you, Charlie. That's why you're not dead. Don't be a silly boy now. If the wizard is there. She goes free. That's a Johnny McCarthy promise.'

31

Charlie waited a few moments to ensure that Johnny was gone before picking up the assault rifle and heading up the stairs.
He turned to look at the magnificent orb that since being hit with Johnny's stray bullet, had begun to make some strange noises: clanking, gurgling, buzzing.
Charlie felt drawn to it as he moved backwards up the steps. As he went to leave, the orb buzzed into life and a bright white light engulfed Charlie.
He saw an image of his daughter, Maddie, wearing her 'Stranger Things' baseball cap and tie dye hoodie. The mage only lasted a moment before the white light faded and the orb fell back into silence. Cahalrie couldn't be sure whether he imagined this moment or what, but he suddenly felt overwhelmed with gratitude, before making his exit.
The car was on Dover Road so he ran towards it, checking his phone on the way. He had a missed call from Maddie, so immediately rang her back.
'Hey dad, I'm en route to Ashford!'
'Oh, really? Your mum let you?'
'Not really, but we need to go get Becky.'
'Wait, what?'
'She's not happy, something strange is going on. I follow her on this new app… and… well I'll tell you when I see you. Pick me up at fifteen at the station!'
'Sure thing.'
Charlie had been here before, bringing Maddie into his world of danger. He had almost lost her, the way he loses everybody close to him.
He would need to be careful, perhaps he could bring

her to the farm and leave her in the car?
Or drop her at his mum's house?
No, he wouldn't have time…
He tried to call Jacko, but there was no answer. As he had his phone in his hand he checked his WhatsApp messages, there was a beautiful photo his mother had sent him of baby Ridley, sleeping.
Well, at least one of his babies would be safe!
Maddie would have to come to the commune with him, as there was no time to lose. Charlie needed to make sure the babies would survive, that Becky would live.
The rest was collateral.
He arrived at the station in Ashford and Maddie, ran to the car and jumped in.
She gave Charlie a big hug, before settling into her seat and putting on her seatbelt.
'So Maddie, there is something we need to do, before we can get home, OK?'
'Sure thing, dad.'
'Don't be alarmed sweetie, I don't want you to be worried but…'
'Becky's missing.'
'Yes… how did you know?' Charlie asked, pulling the car away and heading out of Ashford as quickly as the traffic would let him.
'We have talked about this! I feel things…'
'...Like *Becky* going missing?'
'No, but I can tell when you are sad or anxious. That there's something up. I could tell there was something wrong with Ridley, you know? Your orange turns to black mixed with dark green.'
'Right…'
Maddie looked at Charlie and sighed.

'Listen, dad. I have done some research on this and there are loads of kids out there like me… it's not cool to be like 'oh, well we never had this in my day'... type of thing…'
'Wait, I'm not saying that…'
'It's a genuine thing…'
'I agree! It's like a superpower.' Charlie remembered Tara's words.
Maddie looked at her dad and smiled, proud of him that he wasn't like most adults who dismissed her as a silly girl taking silly talk.
'So, the orange is the new black thing…?' Charlie said, immediately regretting it.
'See, this is what I mean!'
'That came out wrong, Mad. I'm sorry. Tell me about the colours thing again.'
'It's basically that when I think of you and I really concentrate, you are orange. Always. Mum's always green. Tara is… was… wait, sorry…'
'It's OK, Mad. We need to learn to talk about… her. She was what… let me guess…'
'Yellow!' they both said together. Charlie laughed.
'Of course she was!'
'And Becky?'
'What do you think?' Maddie asked.
'Yellow, again?'
'Correct.'
'Honestly, Mad. I love you and I love everything about you…'
'Thanks dad, but as I was saying… you are always orange, because you are half red and half yellow… but when something serious happens, you go black and a bit green.'
Charlie pondered this. He was happy that he was only

half-red. He thought the red might be more like seventy percent but he would take it, that's for sure.
'Anything else? We need to find Becky. Something's wrong. That said...' Maddie got out her phone and checked it, '... oh wait, that's changed?'
'What's changed, sweet?'
'She was showing up on the app as being somewhere near the sea, in the middle of this big green field. We were going in the right direction, but now... she's disappeared.
'Don't worry. I know where we will find her.'
Charlie breathed in deeply as he pulled on to the bypass, proud that together, that between them, they were going to get the job done.
'Hey, Mad. Since we are on the subject of things that are out of the ordinary, what do you think about UFOs?'
'They call them UAP's these days, dad. Unidentified Aerial Phenomena.'
'Oh, right, of course. Do you think that they exist?'
'Are you serious? Of course they exist! You mean to think that we are the only species in the world, and the millions of sightings and experiences with extra-terrestrials are all fake? No way! Also some UAP's are from the multiverse...'
'The multi-what?'
'The multiverse... there are millions of different scenarios playing out alongside each other at the same time. Like a UAP that we think may be from another planet, may actually be from the future or from the past... because time is not linear, like we are told...'
'Is that so?'
'Yeah. I'll explain it to you properly one day.'
Charlie nodded. 'I would love that.'

‘Anyway, what do you think about UAP’s, dad?’
‘Well, I wasn't sure until earlier today. But, now I think they exist. For sure.’
‘What happened today, did you see one?’
‘Something like that.’
‘Come on dad, spill the beans!’
‘I’ll tell you later, we are nearly there.’
Charlie pulled the car off the main drag and onto the slip road that led to the farm. The time was approaching 10am now, so it was daylight, which made Charlie feel slightly more comfortable leaving his daughter.
‘Listen, Mad. I want you to stay here in the car, safe, while I go and investigate. We can lock the doors and you have your phone if there are any problems. OK?’
Charlie checked the phone in her hand and made sure she had battery and at least some signal.
‘But I want to come with!’
‘No way, Maddie. I need you to stay here. I will be back soon with Bex.’
‘But…’
‘No buts. Any problems, who are you going to call?’
‘You.’
‘If you can’t get through to me?’
Maddie paused, ‘999?’
‘Yep, or Jacko. You’ve got his number, right?’
‘Yes, you saved it on my phone last time.’
‘Right, good. I’ll lock the doors and then I’ll be back.’
‘Fine.’
Charlie made sure his dashcam was set to record and then exited the vehicle. He locked it and took a deep breath. He couldn’t quite believe that he was leaving his daughter here, but the only other option was

taking her inside the commune. And what was inside was unknown.
Feeling guilty, but also driven to find Johnny before he did something horrendous, Charlie sprinted from the car and into the woodland before him.
He found the perimeter of the abandoned farm and followed it as quickly as he could before taking the drop down. He could hear the forest coming to life, the cracks of the twigs, the wind in the branches, the rustle of the leaves, he looked back to the top of the ridge to make sure he was not being followed and then continued on towards the tunnel.
The branches had been pulled back and the door was wide open; a sure sign that Johnny was inside.
He continued up the tunnel and towards the second door, which was closed. Charlie opened it quietly and checked to see if there were any signs of life on the other side. He kicked himself for forgetting the gun that was in the boot of the car. The one that the guards had left at the facility, but in his panic he had left it. He wondered whether he should go back, but there was no time to lose.
The commune was quiet. The trees hung over the lodges serenely and Charlie couldn't hear the sound of the fountain in the distance. He moved through the flower arches and towards the courtyard only to find that the fountain was dry. In fact, the faint buzz of life that the commune had, was all but gone.
Charlie immediately thought of the babies. He rushed to the lodge where they slept and barged in through the door.
Light streamed through the windows, but the room was empty. There was nothing left. Charlie had to double-take to make sure this was the correct room,

so went through the door at the end to find once again everything had been cleared out, there was nothing, not one solitary nappy, not one baby bottle.
Out of the final door and back towards the courtyard, it had become clear that the wizard and his subjects had moved on.
As Charlie stood confused, Johnny McCarthy appeared and walked slowly from the opposite side of the courtyard.
'There's no one here, Charlie!' he shouted. 'You told me you left him here!'
'I did, Johnny. I had a choice… I…'
'You fucked it, Charlie. He was here and now he's gone. No sign, no trace.'
'Where's Becky, Johnny?'
'She's long gone, mate. We had a deal. Bring me to the wizard and she gets spared. No Willy the wizard. No Becky.' Johnny said bluntly.
'No! Tell me where she is!' Charlie ordered, moving towards his adversary.
'Now, now. Not a good idea to get all shirty. Remember what happened with your dear Tara!' Johnny said, pulling a revolver from his inside pocket.
Charlie slowed to a halt, a metre or so from the barrel of the gun.
'I'm not sure why I am keeping you alive actually,' Johnny mused, as Charlie begun to raise his hands in the air.
Johnny pushed the gun further towards Charlie's face. He recoiled, dropping to his knees, as Johnny towered above him.
'You need me. You won't find your father without me. I am telling you, Johnny. Don't do it.'

'Thing is, all you do is let people down. You've let *me* down, mate. And I don't know if I can trust you anymore. I think your game is up. You're a bloody burden, you're not a help.'
Johnny cocked the trigger and steeled himself.
'I saw your brother the night you killed him. He had something he wanted to tell you…' Charlie was stalling, trying to buy some time. *But for what?*
'Oh yeah?'
'Yes. Yes, Johnny. He had a message… let me go and we can talk about it…'
'Why don't you just tell me now, eh? Before I lodge this bullet in your brain!' Johnny shouted, smashing Charlie around the face with the gun.
From behind him, Charlie heard movement. Then there was the sound of an assault rifle being fired.
Johnny cowered and in that split second, Charlie dived on top of Johnny, dislodging the gun from his hand.
'Where is Becky? *Where is she?*' Charlie screamed, as his fists reigned down in rage.
'Dad! Dad! Stop!'
The sound of Maddie's voice caused the red mist to ascend and Charlie returned to some semblance of normality. Johnny was unconscious on the floor, danger for now, averted.
Charlie turned to see Maddie holding the assault rifle in her hands.
'Where did you learn to fire that thing?' Charlie said.
'Where do you think, dad? The movies… PlayStation…'
'Right, they didn't teach you how to aim, no?'
'Well, I just wanted to scare him, *obviously.*'
Charlie grabbed Johnny's pistol and took the assault

rifle from Maddie.
'That was very naughty, you were supposed to wait in the car…' Charlie said, feigning anger.
'Whatever, dad.'
Charlie grabbed his daughter and pulled her close to him.
'Thanks, Mad.' he said feeling overwhelmed with emotion.
'Well, I wasn't going to let you go in on your own, was I?' Maddie smiled.

32

'There is a future, Charlie. I want you to know that.' Tara stated. She sat with her knees tucked into her chest as she always used to. She was wearing a black top and her blue jeans. She looked like she usually did.

She looked beautiful.

'Really?'

'Yeah, of course. Even if you can't see it yet.'

Charlie looked down at the sea gently lapping the shore. The hills in the distance framed this scene perfectly and the pink clouds provided the icing on the cake.

'But, I don't know where she is?'

'It may not feel like it, but it doesn't matter.'

'What if she's dead... what if she's in pain...'

Tara cocked her head to one side and smiled.

'You're an empath, Charlie. Perhaps you need to stop spending time worrying about everybody else and focus on you. Focus on our children.'

'Well, that's easier said than done. Also, how am I going to cope without you?'

'You have enough strong women in your life, Charlie. You will be fine!'

'Is Ridley going to be OK?'

'Who knows, Charlie? But she has got more chance with you around to bring her up.'

'OK.'

'You are a good man, Charlie. You may not believe it and you may have made some mistakes. But I know you, and I love you.'

'Can you stay with me?'

'You know I can't, Charlie.'

'Please?'
Tara smiled and then disappeared into the clouds. Charlie sat alone, looking out at the beautiful view.

The sound of sheep woke Charlie from slumber.
His eyes felt wet but inside he felt strong, happy.
The sun streamed through the curtains, so he opened them fully to embrace the wonderful view.
He loved his mum's house. From the spare bedroom window he looked out onto a field of sheep. The well-manicured garden sat below; roses, dahlias, rhododendrons.
The door opened behind him.
'Yes! Dad's up!' Maddie shouted, before coming in and giving Charlie a hug.
'Did you sleep well, kiddo?'
'Yep. Did you? It's nearly 9am, even I'm awake before you today!'
'I guess so. Right, give me five minutes and I'll get showered and come down.'
'I'll tell granny to put the coffee on!'
'Thanks, Mad.'
Charlie jumped in the shower and got changed.
The house was still and quiet, calm and peaceful. For the first time in a while he felt good, at peace.
Perhaps it was the dream he had. Perhaps he had gone some way to forgiving himself for all of the loss, all of the tragedy.
He padded along the upstairs hallway and down to the ground floor. The kitchen lay to his left, the dining room to his right and the large living room in front of him. The door was slightly ajar, so he pushed it to see his mother in her armchair, knitting, while Maddie sat watching 'The Vampire Diaries' on Netflix.

‘Hello, sleepyhead.’ his mother said.
‘Hi,’ Charlie said, heading straight to Ridley. She was warm and cosy in her blanket, stirring. Her eyes kept opening and then closing at the sound of the TV, so Charlie turned it down slightly much to Maddie’s disappointment.
Charlie gave Ridley a big hug. He thought she smiled, but maybe it was just wind… *babies can’t smile at this age. Surely?*
He put her back down in the cot and stroked her head.
‘Your coffee is brewing on the side.’
‘Thanks, mum.’
Charlie went through to the kitchen next door and pressed the plunger on the cafetiere.
‘Hey, dad?’ came a whisper from behind him.
‘Yes, Maddie?’
‘Yeah… I just wanted to say that… I think Becky’s alive.’
‘Yes, darling of course Becky is alive! Don’t be so silly,’ Charlie said trying to play down the potential seriousness of Becky’s predicament.
‘Come on, dad. I’m not a baby. I know you are dealing with some serious bad guys. I mean, take that guy you fought yesterday, he was going to shoot you. WITH A GUN! Good thing Maddie was there to save the day and we could watch him get arrested!’
‘Yes, indeed darling. He won’t be out on the streets for a very long time…’
‘Hopefully forever… Here, dad. Why didn’t you call Jacko, your mate, to come and arrest him? That’s what you usually do?’
‘Erm… well I did, but for some reason he hasn’t been answering his calls. Perhaps he is busy chasing other

bad guys.'
Charlie got a spoon and stirred his drink.
'Anyway, about Becky. She is alive and I think she is OK. I think she is hiding. Somewhere. I feel... blue-green. No black. She's OK...'
Charlie took a sip of coffee. The black liquid burnt the back of his throat a little.
'You know, it's funny. I think she is OK too.' Charlie said.
'What makes you think that?'
'I don't know, just a hunch.'
'We need to go and find her. And before you start dad, I'm not too young, it's not too dangerous... I can help.'
'Yeah, on that note, does your mother know you are here?'
'I told her last night that I was sleeping at granny's.'
'Good. Good. When does she want you back?'
'Tomorrow, latest.'
'Oh, cool. We could go to West Ham today. If you like?'
'Yeah, we got Leeds today.'
'Correct.'
'Or, we could find Becky... she can't have gone far.'
There was a nagging, longing in Charlie's heart.
'I suppose we could stop by some of the places she may be. There is definitely one place in Folkestone that she could be holding up...'
'.... Or at the police station and see if anything has been filed. Missing persons... or see if there may be any information?'
Charlie nodded and from the next room, Ridley started wailing.
'I'll make some milk. You head back to granny.'

Charlie pondered the dilemma once more of his daughter being involved in something even he didn't fully understand.
She may be 12 going on 21, but this was a bridge too far. It would be down to him to find Becky, it was his job. Although he had no idea where she was. She was nowhere to be found at the commune. After they had disarmed Johnny McCarthy and waited for the police to find the place, they then searched the area thoroughly and there was absolutely no sign of human life. *None whatsoever.* After forty years of communal living. Well at least that's what the police and authorities said.
Charlie brought the milk from the kitchen and took Ridley in his arms.
'You see the prime minister has apologised for his outrageous party last year?' his mum said, turning the page on the newspaper she was reading.
'Well about time. Here Mad, can you go upstairs and grab my phone from the side of the bed. Thank you!'

With a harrumph, Maddie heaved herself from the sofa.
'I think his days are numbered, quite frankly!' his mother continued.
Charlie smiled and nodded as his mum placed the paper down.
'How is the little one getting on?' She said, 'give her here, I'll finish her feed.'
His mother thrust her arms out and took the baby. As much as Charlie was enjoying being a dad for once, he thought it best not to argue.
He heard Maddie's heavy steps come down the stairs as he waited for his phone.

'Dad, check your messages…' she said, her eyes wide and face shocked.
Charlie had one unread message:

Hi Charlie, I'm safe. I can't tell you precisely where I am right now, but I need you to know. I'm safe. Don't try and find me. Seriously, Charlie. I will find you when I can. xxx

Maddie nodded at Charlie, and mouthed the words, 'she's alive.' Charlie smiled and Maddie danced her little happy dance.
Charlie's phone rang with an unknown number. Maddie stopped dancing.
'Come next door, Mad.'
'Don't you want to answer that…?' his mother called as they left the room, Charlie with the phone ringing in his hand. He had got rid of his voicemail service, so it would ring indefinitely if someone really wanted him, or until he decided to cut it off.
'Maddie, whatever happens, I want you to stay here and make sure granny and Ridley are safe. OK? Then when you can, get granny to take you back to your mum, yeah?'
'Yeah, but… I don't feel good, dad…'
The phone kept ringing…
'Are you going to answer that, Charlie?' His mum called from the other room.
'I know. Listen, I love you. It's going to be OK. But this time, don't come after me, OK? I really mean it this time.'
Maddie nodded, holding her tummy.
'Next time you see me, I will be with Becky and we will go to West Ham together, I promise.'

The phone continued to ring…
'Answer the bloody phone!'
'I love you, Mad.'
'I love you too, dad.'
'Go and stay with granny. Tell her I had to go.'
'OK, dad.'
Charlie walked out of the front door and pressed the green button on his phone.
'Hello, Charlie. Well done for sorting that out with… Madison is it? That's fine. We don't have any interest in your mother or your daughters. But we do need to talk to *you.*'
Charlie didn't recognise the voice.
'If you just keep walking around the corner and in the distance you will see a black car…'
Charlie continued walking out of the cul-de-sac where his mother lived and saw a large, black Mercedes parked along the small, country lane.
He thought about running…across the field… into the bushes? *Then what?*
'Yep, not worth it Charlie. Let's just have a little chat, get in the car and no-one else needs to get hurt, OK?'
'Who is this?'
'Just get in the car, Charlie.'
Charlie Stone walked towards the black car. A lady in a black suit and sunglasses got out of the passenger seat and opened the back door for him.
Charlie Stone got in, and after a few moments, the car slowly pulled away.

EPILOGUE

1983, somewhere near the Romney Marsh

'There's not a way to do it, I told you.'
'Yes, but if we all had that attitude then we wouldn't have... I don't know... the lightbulb... or the TV? Or...'
'Listen, Will... if you could use electromagnetic force to control inanimate objects then I will eat this hat.'
Rob took the hat off his head and pretended to take a big bite out of it. Both men laughed.
'You know, it is peaceful down here.'
'That it is. So much better than being in London.'
'Don't say that!'
'Well, you know what I mean.'
'Anyway, have you finished that gasper? You do know you can smoke inside the pub, right?'
'Of course, but there is something about the cool breeze and the nicotine mixed together that gives me a little buzz.'
'You are either ahead of your time or a bit of a weirdo, mate.'
'Funny, you are not the first person to say that. Especially the weirdo bit. Come on let's get inside.'

Rob went to the bar and ordered two more pints while Will was at the jukebox putting on some tracks.
The first song came on, 'Always on my Mind, ny Elvis Presley.
'Gosh, you do love this song, don't you will?'
'Yes, yes I do. And you know why, don't you?'
'Go on, do tell me once more...'
'It's the song that was playing when I first met you.

When we first got together and when we first started. Well…. this…'
'Whatever *this* is…'
'They say you must never mix work with pleasure, but I guess we have done more than our fair share of that!'
'Be careful, you don't know who might be listening. It's not as… open-minded shall we say, down here…' Rob said, checking over his shoulder.
'You know, what you were saying the other day…'
'Oh, really? This again? I thought you would wait until we had at least five pints…'
'No, but think about it. If sarge was keen, and I mean *really* keen to move things along then we could start the process soon…'
'Will, seriously, I am more about the magnets… rather than the… ' Rob looked either side of him again, 'the chemical nerve agents…'
'Yes, I know but hear me out. We have a place. Near here, I want to show you.' Will said eagerly.
'What do you mean, *we* do? What the army?'
Will nodded.
'Really?'
Will nodded again.
'It's only small, limited funding, but it's a start. Maybe you could come on board with me and work on your physicsy… doctor-stuff…'
'Show me.'
The men finished their pints and walked to Rob's car. Will directed Rob deeper into the Marsh.
'That's the beauty of being out here… dead. Not like London, no-one gives a toss what we are up to.'
'Maybe, Will. Maybe.'
Behind them, there was a sudden flash of brilliant

white light. The car swerved to the left violently and Rob brought the car to a halt.
'What the hell was that?'
'God knows…'
The men exited the vehicle and turned towards the coast.
Hovering just above sea level was a large orb, pulsing gold, it was like nothing they had ever seen before.
'Jesus, that's not…'
'It's like a whale… but gold…'
'And above the sea…'
'But it's breathing, no?'
'It, God knows…'
The orb moved sharply, swiftly over their head and stopped suddenly.
'It's stopped over our facility…'
'What's it doing?'
'Wait… it's no longer glowing.'
The hum and whirr and whoosh of the vessel suddenly faltered and it dropped around twenty metres down from the sky.
'It's… crashing?'
'Quick, get to cover!'
The men ran as the craft wobbled, faltered and hit the ground, not with a smash, but with a thud and was silent.

Yesterday, 2022, Sunny Sands Beach.

'Robert's dead, you know.'
'Yes. As is my son, Steve.'
'Johnny is in custody, too.'
The wizard looked out to sea, watching the waves break against the rocks that framed Folkestone

Harbour.
'Is it over, then? The project?'
'No, Willy. You know that they are looking into moving Operation 'Born Again'. It's already in play. The subjects are in transit as we speak.'
The wizard paused. He picked up a seashell, then threw it away.
'Rob's work... what's happening with that?'
'I think they want to move it all to one secure location.'
'But I can't do it without Rob. We have been partners for forty years.'
Darren Jackson smiled at Willy. 'Listen, I know how close you two were. I mean, I have kept it a secret for everyone's sake, but I know it must be hard for you.'
William McCarthy shot DCI Jackson a cold, hard look and changed the subject.
'What about the Stone guy. Charlie? I should have got rid of him when I had the chance. He knows about the operation, all of it.'
'Yes, he does.' Jacko confirmed.
'And he is your friend. I can see why. There is something... it's difficult to describe isn't it? But there is something about him.' the wizard mused, staring Jacko straight in the eye.
Jacko looked down at the sand.
'He was my friend. I don't really... it's not an issue anymore.'
The wizard nodded.
'Looks like your ride is here.' Jacko said, looking over his shoulder and up towards the harbour. There was a black Mercedes perched by the side of the road. Waiting.
'And they will take me to the new operation?' the

wizard asked.
'That's what I have been told.'
The wizard got up and flicked the sand from his white garments.
'Thanks Detective Inspector Jackson, you know your work here, your confidentiality, has been very much in the public interest.'
'I understand and it's not my place to challenge the status quo. I just follow the orders, Will.'
The wizard smiled and nodded.
'Thanks again.'
The wizard walked slowly to the waiting car, and Jacko watched him get in.
As the door closed behind him, Jacko walked down the beach. He had finished his shift but had an hour or so until he needed to pick his kids up from school.
He took his shoes and socks off, letting the cold water wash over his feet. Charlie was right, police work was just a load of lies, bureaucracy, protecting the elite and maybe once in a few months or so, solving a crime.
Still, it paid the bills.
Jacko headed back towards the harbour, maybe he could stop in for a pint before the school run.
When he turned the corner, back past the rocks, he noticed that the black car was still there, engine purring at the side of the road. The rear window was open and a pair of eyes were still staring at him.
How odd, Jacko thought. *Why haven't they left yet?*
'Sorry, Detective.' came a voice from behind him.
The silencer on the pistol prevented any attention from being drawn to the beach, as Detective Inspector Darren Jackson dropped to the sandy carpet.
A few moments later, the rear window closed and the

black Mercedes disappeared into the Folkestone afternoon.

THE END

SUNNY SANDS

An absorbing and powerful thriller from a gritty, modern voice. A teenage body washed up on the beach... A twisted operation conceived by criminal masterminds... DS Charlie Stone is struggling. Recently separated from his wife and estranged from his daughter Maddie, Charlie is trying hard to keep his life together. An apparently cut and dried case of murder piques Charlie's interest. As he delves further into the murky coastal underworld, he realises things are darker than they first appeared. Charlie's family become being dragged into a world of darkness, danger and depravity. Can Charlie find the answers, while keeping all he holds dear, safe from harm?
For fans of Lee Child and Ian Rankin.

CRIMSON CROSS

The second novel in the Charlie Stone series... A dark, intricate network is spreading through Europe... Teenager's murdered in draconian ways... Charlie Stone's most formidable enemy yet... From the backstreets of Hamburg to the archaic village of Grund in Luxembourg, a startling sequence of terrifying murders will push Charlie Stone to his mental and physical limits. Incarcerated in Police Protection, DS Stone is frustrated. Despite Amy Green's killers being brought to justice, a gruesome murder in Hawkinge is a stark reminder that the case is far from closed. In an attempt to find the perpetrators, Charlie is sent across Europe before heading back to Folkestone for a final showdown with his arch-nemesis. Will Charlie be able to keep his family together as all hell breaks loose in his working life? Will he be able to connect the dots before the murders start to become personal? Can Charlie keep those he loves safe whilst struggling against his most powerful adversary yet?

TWO WOLVES

Darkness descends on Charlie Stone as he finds himself separated from his fiancée Tara, and estranged from his daughter Maddie. As Charlie turns to the demon drink for solace, he finds himself sinking deeper into an abyss of loneliness, isolation and despair. When the case he has been chasing is dropped, Charlie Stone goes rogue. With the aid of his wayward friend, Robbie, Charlie seeks to bring the demons from his past to justice, in any way possible. This dark gritty, urban thriller twists and turns until its eye-opening climax. But, can Charlie conquer his inner demons before they destroy him?

Printed in Great Britain
by Amazon

76918759R00149